NO EASY ANSWERS

No Easy Answers

Carolyn Hart

ISBN: 979-8-3372-0398-0

This edition published in 2026 by Open Road Integrated Media, Inc.
180 Maiden Lane
New York, NY 10038
www.openroadmedia.com

To Mel and Dorothy Hart

NO EASY ANSWERS

A TOUGH MOB

It was a tough mob waiting for us. I knew somebody was going to get hurt when I saw its leader. He had curly black hair and a zealot's face, tightly drawn and savage. He was waving his arms and yelling, "Let's show these dirty Commies where to get off. We don't have to stand for it!" Still shouting, he led the charge. He was a real *über-alles* type.

I shoved Nancy behind me and threw up my left arm. A bald-headed, fat man in dungarees was bearing down on us, a two-by-four raised high. The big brave America-Firsters had come prepared. Bottles smashed. Somebody screamed over at the edge of the square. Close by a woman wept, "No, please, nor I was trying to knock this fat toad in the stomach, but Nancy was pulling on my back, crying, "Bart! Come on! Quick, let's get out of here."

I pulled free of her and swung around, but not fast enough. The rock slammed into the side of my head and I was down on my knees. Somebody kicked me in the ribs and I fell on my face.

The crowd swirled around, people crying and shouting, and over it all I could hear the high-pitched squeal of the mob's leader.

"That's it. Give 'em hell. We'll send 'em back where they came from!"

The sirens shrilled as the cop cars slewed around the corner. The yells were louder now. The peace marchers were falling back, trying to run away from the rocks and bottles and clubs and bricks.

The main action had moved into the center of the square and it had the nightmare quality of split scenes in a Panavision super-special—but what made it a nightmare was that it was real. The screams meant somebody hurt. The blood was warm and fresh and brightly red in the soft light of the summer evening. The hate was hard and ugly—a two-by-four cracking against bone.

I was up on my hands and knees again and trying to scramble to my feet. And then I got sick. I threw up all over me and Nancy, who was trying to get me back on my feet. After a long shuddering minute, I did get up.

"Sorry," I muttered. "I guess my head. . . ." Then I shut up. My head hurt, sure, but that wasn't the reason I got sick.

Nancy didn't say anything, she just reached out for my hand. She understood. She held tight to my hand for an instant, then started tugging.

"Bart, we've got to get out of here! Come on, we can cut down this alley."

I stood there, unsteadily, and sick at my stomach and mad and scared. Then I saw this big bruiser, some guy about six foot two and built like Sam Huff, and he had Father Rosser up against the side of a big oak tree and he was beating him down into the ground.

I pulled free from Nancy and started swearing and yelling and running, but the crowd milled in front of me. Then one of the cops saw what was happening and got there first and yanked this big guy around and knocked him down.

More tires squealed and I saw the green of Military Police

cars. They jolted to a stop and then men spilled out. I knew it would be over in a minute. The police had called on the post for help and it wouldn't take the MPs long to handle it.

I hesitated, but there wasn't anything we could do. For anybody. It was all over and we'd better get out of there before some MP who knew us spotted us. Dusk was falling but it wasn't quite dark yet.

We ran into the alley. I held Nancy's arm as we skirted around garbage cans and stepped over tangled boards. Broken glass crunched under our feet.

"It's pretty rotten. To have to leave."

"Oh Bart, we did have to! We couldn't get picked up in that kind of mess. Our folks are pretty decent about our working in the peace movement at all."

It was three more blocks, three more long, dirty alleys, until we got to Prospect, where I'd parked the car earlier. It seemed like another lifetime. We had been laughing when we got out of the car. I was teasing Nancy, because she was so conservatively dressed. A skirt and blouse and sweater. No bellbottom pantsuit or go-go boots.

"Father Rosser was pretty definite about it last night," she responded. "He doesn't want the marchers to look like Yippies. And I notice you aren't sporting your peace beads tonight."

"I just do that to bug my dad."

It had all seemed pretty funny a couple of hours ago. Our neat clothes and Father Rosser's warning that marchers—any kind of marchers—faced danger and perhaps even death.

But not here, of course. Not in Stockton. I'd have bet my life on that or I wouldn't have let Nancy come.

I opened the car door for her, then walked around and climbed in behind the wheel. I put the key in the ignition, then my hand dropped.

"I'm going back."

Nancy grabbed my arm.

"Bart, you can't. You'll be picked up or the MPs will see you."

"I don't care," I said bitterly. "Father Rosser's hurt and I ran away. It's wrong. All wrong. A bunch of seminarians and some college kids and some middle-aged League-of-Women-Voters types get out to have a march. We even had a permit from the mayor. And look what happens! Bully boys with clubs and bricks. It isn't like the marchers were a bunch of thugs. Nobody was yelling dirty words or throwing anything. It was just people marching."

"The police came and stopped the mob. There's nothing you can do now."

"I can go back and tell the police what I saw."

"You might be picked up, too. You knocked down that fat man."

I opened the car door. "So, I'm picked up."

She held on to me tighter. "You know what Dad's policy is."

I sat there. Yes, I knew what Major General Martin Loring's policy was. Any post resident arrested by the Stockton police faced banishment from the post as an "undesirable dependent". And if he didn't boot me, he would get catcalls from all sides—because I dated the general's daughter. And it would be a black mark on my father's record and he was up for promotion to brigadier general.

I slammed shut the car door and started the engine without a word. We drove east on Prospect then turned north on Pershing Avenue, the main road into the post. Two miles later I stopped at the guarded gates into the post to show our IDs. Only persons with post IDs or official passes are permitted into Fort Calhoun. It's a highly restricted area.

The MP flashed his light on my ID then into the car. The light wavered then fastened on my face.

"You hurt, buddy?"

"I fell down."

He checked my ID again, looked at Nancy's, then handed them back and waved us on.

"He'll remember me when word of the riot hits the post," I said.

"I'll say we were on a picnic out at Lake Buren and that you stumbled over some rocks and. . . ."

"Nancy," I said quietly. I glanced at her and in the soft light from the dash she looked at me and shrugged.

"Women," I said. "I think you'd lie to the Angel Gabriel if you thought it would help one of your own and you figured you had half a chance to get away with it."

"That's right," she said evenly.

What could I say?

Pershing Avenue swept through a forest of pine trees for about three miles before you reached the post buildings. We passed a clump of barracks and then a mess hall. Rinky-tink piano sounded from the noncommissioned officers' club. Just past it, Grant Street veered east from Pershing. I swung onto Grant and slowed the car. On either side of the road, family housing spread, officers' to the north and NCOs' to the south.

The Army doesn't provide grand quarters for anybody except the commanding general. The quarters are nice and on the older posts sometimes beautiful in a nostalgic antebellum way.

Fort Calhoun, like the Army itself, was a mixture of the old and the new. Lieutenants and captains lived in Capehart housing, suburban-type duplexes with two or three bedrooms. We wound past the homes, all alike even to the shabby station wagons and sticker-laden VWs parked along the curbs.

Then Grant Avenue began to climb and curve among gentle hills. Lights gleamed up on the ridge to our left. The officers' club. Faint strains of music sounded and we could hear laughter and the splash of water from the pool.

Once past the club, Grant skirted the edge of a river. To the left, above hilly well-kept lawns, were the rambling two-story homes of the lieutenant colonels and bird colonels. My house, the quarters of Colonel Michael Hastings, was lighted downstairs. As we passed, I looked for Dad's car but didn't see it. I hoped he was home. He'd come in late last night and left before I was up this morning. Some big maneuver going on, I guessed. But I'd wait up for him tonight, because I was going to have it out with my folks.

I guess I pushed a little harder on the accelerator, because Nancy cautioned me.

"Better slow down, Bart. Remember, you're back on the post."

"Yeah. Back in the all-smothering womb."

"Just for the summer," she said soothingly.

"Not even that, honey. I'm going to haul my carcass right back to the campus. Tomorrow. I should go to summer school anyway. It's not too late to enroll."

We were at the end of Grant then and high on a hilltop stood the quarters of the post commander. I turned into the circular graveled drive. Nancy was home.

I pulled up by the front door, turned off the motor, and faced Nancy.

"Do you have any idea what kind of hypocrite I feel like?" I asked miserably. "All year on the campus I helped in the drive to get people to sign the petition for a volunteer army. Then I come back to the post and I'm a colonel's son, and all his friends keep asking me why don't I try for an appointment to the Point. 'You've got good grades, son, and you made the football team as a freshman. The kind of a man we need.'"

I looked at Nancy. In the soft light shading out from her front porch, her hair was the gold of honey and just as soft and flowing. I reached out and gently twined my fingers in it, then my hand dropped away and curled into a fist.

"I feel like the biggest phony in the world. And I don't say anything. I can't tell some colonel that I think he's thrown his life away, that he's been conned. All this Keep-America-Free stuff. The Red Menace. The Communist Threat."

I flexed the fingers of my hand and I could feel the muscles move. Alive and living, that was me. But so many were dead.

"Kyle bought the whole package," I said bitterly. "He went to the Point. Mom and Dad were really proud of him. A cadet colonel. The whole business."

And Kyle really had been the whole business. All my life. He was the brother you'd want to match. He'd had bright-red hair, and freckles spattered all over his face, and a grin that made the world a fun place to be.

But Kyle didn't live to laugh for very long. He was three days past twenty-four when the Vietcong overran his platoon and Kyle's M-16 jammed. And it was goodbye Kyle.

Abruptly I reached out for Nancy's hand. "I'm sorry. I should keep my mouth shut."

She was staring out the windshield, but I knew she wasn't looking at the night. A lot of Army people have buried their own, this last war.

"Tommy believed in what he was doing," she said, and I could hear the tears in her voice. I wasn't the only one who had loved a big brother.

"He kept writing about the people. He helped set up a dispensary for the Montagnard children." She stopped and her hand tightened in mine. "He was a good soldier."

"A good soldier," I repeated tiredly. "Maybe if we didn't have so many good soldiers, the U.S. would keep out of some wars. This Red Threat business, it makes me sick!"

Neither of us said anything more for a little while, then Nancy sighed and pushed her hair back from her face.

"What are you going to do, Bart?"

"I'm going home and I'm going to tell Dad that I was in the riot and that I've had enough of lying—because that's what it is when you just stand there and make small talk and don't yell it to the world that you'd never go to the Point. That's what I'm going to do."

Nancy opened the car door and got out and shut it. Then she leaned in the open window and her voice was tired and sad.

"Don't do it, Bart. If you leave them like this, if you throw it up to them that Kyle died for nothing, it will break their world to pieces."

THE SEARCH

But I was going to slay my dragon that night. I wasn't going to put it off for another hour. Barton MacDonald Hastings II was through with the phony bit.

When I pulled into our drive, I slammed out of my Mustang in a hurry. The sooner it was done, the better. And then when I got inside and skidded to a stop in the doorway to the living room, I saw that only Mom was there.

"Isn't Dad home?" I asked.

Mother laid down her book and looked toward the hallway where I stood in the shadow.

"No, dear. I've scarcely seen him since Wednesday. Some problem with the shipment of M-18s. It must be serious but he hasn't said what's happened."

I suddenly felt like a windup toy that's unwound. I was all braced for the big confrontation and only Mom was there. I walked tiredly on into the room. Mother's smile of welcome froze then slid away.

"Barton, what's happened to you?"

I was still all wrapped up in my idea of having it out with Dad, so I just looked blankly at her for a minute.

"Your head!" she exclaimed. "Your clothes! Barton, have you had a wreck?"

I looked down at my best brown slacks. The right knee was ripped out, and dirt and grass stains were smeared all over the front of them. And throwing up hadn't helped their appearance, either. My shirt was ripped, too, and the side of my head ached. I put up my hand and could feel the dirt and blood.

"No, Mom, I didn't have a wreck. I just happened to be on the wrong side at the peace rally."

Her face changed in an instant. Mom hates peace marchers because of Kyle.

"You marched?" she asked, and her voice was cool and stiff.

I walked over and eased down into an overstuffed chair.

"Yeah, me and Nancy Loring and about twenty seminarians and a couple of priests and some housewives. But the clods who sing "The Star Spangled Banner" the loudest at the football games, they don't think anybody has a right to be free but them."

"What are you talking about, Barton?"

I leaned back in the chair and stared at the ceiling. "I'm talking about all those patriotic lovers of democracy who want to beat you to a pulp if you disagree with them. A mob of 'em, complete with bricks and boards, charged us in the square. A lot of people got hurt before the police and the MPs broke it up."

Mother's gentle face was set and angry, and she bit off her words. "You really have it all figured out, don't you, Barton? You sneer at your country, but the police and the MPs came and saved you. You do have the right to march and to believe as you wish. But you don't want to admit that, do you? It's easier to sneer."

"In a lot of places, it's been the police who've beaten up the marchers," I shot back.

She nodded. "That's right, but they're censured for it. We

aren't a police state yet—but it will come to that if you peace-loving marchers have your way."

"That's a lie!" I said hotly. "The people who march want peace and freedom!"

"That's what they want. But they aren't willing to defend it." She rose from the couch and walked toward the hall. At the doorway, she stopped and looked back and said bitterly, so bitterly, "If you want to march, if you love your country, why don't you march in the memory of Americans who died for it? Like your brother."

And she looked at me as she would at a stranger.

I was angry and hurt and my voice was thick in my throat when I shouted, "It's a lie, a rotten lie! Kyle didn't die to defend his country. He died because of a bogey—the Communist Threat. Anytime we want to control some territory, keep it on our side, we run the same old garbage up the flagpole—resist Communist Aggression. Oh sure! Save Vietnam for the Vietnamese. Do you know how many Vietnamese we've killed by saving them? How many women and children we've burned up with napalm bombs? How many—"

"Shut up."

I stood there, shaking inside with anger and hurt. My mother had never said that to me in my life.

"You do know everything, don't you, Barton?" she said harshly. "You've learned so much this first year away from home. So there's no Communist threat! You must be sure and tell that to the Czechs and the Hungarians and the Poles and the East Berliners and the Tibetans. There are so many people who would be so happy to share in your wisdom."

And we stood there, hating each other.

The only people who can wound you, really cut you deep, are the ones you love. And when you quarrel it cuts and tears and destroys.

I took a step forward and held out my hand. "I'm sorry, Mom. I didn't mean it about Kyle."

Her face crumpled and she swung around and hurried through the door into the hallway.

She didn't stop when the hard pounding knock came at the front door. I started to go after her, but the insistent thud at the door was urgent, demanding. Still I hesitated, watching Mother run up the stairs, but the knocking was louder, heavier.

"Just a minute," I called. I took a deep breath, trying to get steady again, but the knocking kept right on. It made me mad.

I crossed to the door and threw it open.

I said, "Just a minute! What do you. . . ?"

Then I saw the brass, a colonel and a major. Standing behind them were a couple of sergeants carrying attaché cases.

"What's the matter?" I asked. "What's wrong?" Because I knew immediately that something was wrong.

"Is your mother home, Barton? We'd like to speak to her." I recognized him then. It was Colonel Griswold, the provost marshal.

"Yes," I said uncertainly. "Come in."

When they stepped into the entryway, I was even surer that something was really wrong. Colonel Griswold, an old golfing buddy of Dad's, he seemed—well—almost embarrassed.

I gripped his arm. "Colonel, has something happened to Dad?"

He wouldn't meet my eyes. "It's just a precaution," he said, and he almost seemed to be talking to himself. "It's ridiculous, but I can't—"

"Not ridiculous, sir," the major interrupted. "It's the clear implication from the facts. And we've already held off longer than we should. It looked bad on Wednesday. We've held off for two days. That's long enough."

I looked from one to the other, from the short, dapper major, his uniform a perfect fit, to the big, bulky colonel, and I didn't know what they were talking about.

"What's going on?" I asked.

The colonel fastened his eyes on the chandelier that hung from the hall ceiling. "Call your mother, Barton, that's a good boy."

"She's not feeling very well, sir," I began, and then I paused. The major was looking at me and I could have sworn he looked satisfied, pleased even, when I said that. "She's—"

And then Mother called down from the hall landing, "That's all right, Barton." She came down the stairs, her face composed, her auburn hair sleek and shining. And she had a welcoming smile on her face.

"Bill, how nice to see you. What can I do to help you?"

And the colonel was obviously embarrassed. He looked everywhere but at my mother and his voice was muffled and his face flushed.

"Celia, I'm damn sorry about this, but I don't really have a choice. I know something's screwy somewhere, but everything points to Mike. I just had to follow it up as if it weren't Mike involved at all. I hope you can understand."

"Bill, what are you trying to say?" Mother asked quietly.

The colonel stared at the parquet flooring. Its light and dark interlocking squares gleamed with polish. Then he looked up at my mother, an appeal in his eyes. "I hope you'll understand, Celia. It's just a formality. But once the quarters are searched, it will help show that Mike didn't have anything to do with it."

"Didn't have anything to do with what?" Mother demanded.

The colonel faced Mother squarely this time and the embarrassment dropped away from him. Instead, he was a very worried man. "The M-18. The new rifle Mike's in charge of testing, Celia. An M-18 disappeared Wednesday and Mike's the only one who could have taken it—at least, that's what Major Wiley's investigation shows. So that's why we're here."

Mother's face flushed. Her clear green eyes, the color of sea water, were cold with fury. She looked from the colonel to the major and back again. "Where's Mike now?"

"Mike's okay," the colonel answered hastily. "He's down at the CID office, going over it and over it. He says the whole thing's either a mistake or a frame-up. He told us to come right on over and search. I believe him, Celia, but the rifle is gone."

"Even if it is, I don't see. . . ." Mother began angrily. Then she broke off and said shortly, "Search if you wish." She turned away and walked into the living room.

Colonel Griswold hurried after her. "Celia, I'm real sorry, but don't you see, this will prove it's a mare's nest."

She faced him. "That shouldn't need proof."

Colonel Griswold looked away and said sharply to the major, "All right. Get started."

Major Wiley said, "Yes, sir," crisply, but he made no move. Instead, he looked slowly around the living room.

It was like so many officers' quarters on posts around the world—the furniture a little shabby, scarred from so many moves; a few beautiful things—a mahogany coffee table from the Philippines, a massive, carved grandfather clock from Germany, a Japanese screen painting. And, here and there, an odd piece of quartermaster furniture, an easy chair, a sideboard, a sofa, the extra pieces available on posts to help Army people stretch that tight budget a little further.

It was a comfortable room. This room or one like it in so many places around the world had spelled home all my life, always a temporary home but, in a way, an unchanging one. A haven. A happy place to be.

That night it looked like a pasteboard set. It was all unreal—my mother standing there so stiff and straight, the colonel staring unhappily at the floor, the major carefully studying the lair of his quarry. And, waiting quietly in the hall, two hard-faced CID sergeants.

Major Wiley was slick, young for his rank. His bristly crew cut was blond, his face narrow and intelligent—and his pale-blue eyes didn't miss anything. They fastened finally on the open door to the den.

"Does the colonel keep his personal records in there, ma'am?" he asked. His voice was deferential enough, but determined.

"Yes."

"With your permission then, ma'am, we will begin our search there." And he nodded at the two sergeants.

Mother stood still and quiet in the center of the living room. Colonel Griswold touched her arm apologetically. "If you don't mind, Celia, we'd like for you to watch so there won't be any question of—anything," he finished lamely.

Mother made no answer but she turned and walked into the den.

I couldn't believe it was happening. The CID couldn't be searching my dad's desk, suspecting him of stealing a rifle. My dad was a full colonel. He had been nominated to be a brigadier general. This had to be some kind of crazy mistake!

But it was happening. I moved to the doorway of the den. The major crisply directed the sergeants. Then, pulling on a pair of gloves, he began to search Dad's desk.

It was bad but I took it until he pulled open the top drawer on the right and lifted out a packet of letters from Kyle.

I lunged across the den and grabbed the letters.

"You can't touch these! These are Dad's letters from Kyle. What kind of rotten Gestapo—"

"Kyle?" the major interrupted. "Who's he?"

"My brother. My dead brother. He was West Point and he was killed in Vietnam, and now you and your storm troopers paw through his letters like you had a right to. You don't have—"

"That's enough, Barton," Mother said quietly. "Let him look. Nothing can hurt Kyle anymore."

I looked at her and I wanted to kick the slick major in the stomach. Maybe nobody could hurt Kyle, but they could sure hurt my mother. Her eyes were fastened on Kyle's letters and then she looked up at me and I guess she knew what I was going to do because she put out her hand and said sharply, "No, Barton, let them look. The sooner they look, the sooner they'll leave."

The major was watching me, his eyes bright and interested. I thrust the letters back at him. He took them and still he looked at me.

"You been in a fight?"

"No."

The older sergeant looked up briefly from the fireplace. "A riot in town, sir. Some peace marchers ran into some bricks. Lieutenant McCory and his men helped break it up."

The major nodded. "Peace marchers," he repeated softly. He looked me over good again, then bent back to the desk. He emptied each drawer, checked the contents, then tapped the drawer inside and out before flipping it over to look at the bottom.

He finished with the side drawers and pulled out the broad shallow center drawer. It was Standard Operating Procedure, until he flipped the drawer over. He tensed like a bird dog on point.

"McIntosh," he said sharply.

The sergeant swung around from the fireplace and was across

the room quicker than I'd have thought such a big man could move.

Everybody crowded close to the desk.

"Stand back," the major ordered. "Get a picture first, Mcintosh."

The sergeant reached for his attaché case, opened it, and pulled out a thirty-five-millimeter Leica, equipped with flash. He took a half-dozen shots.

Then Major Wiley bent over the upturned drawer and gently began to loosen the tape that held a small blue-backed booklet to the wood.

Mother, her face puzzled and worried, moved near. Then she sighed with relief. "That's just our bankbook, Major. I don't know why Mike put it there, but. . . ."

The major waved her to silence and again I wanted to kick him. I wanted to knock him down and grind his narrow face into the floor.

He had the booklet free now. He held it by the edges, opening the pages with a gloved fingertip. I watched contemptuously. The Gestapo sure liked to run it out.

The major stopped at one page and studied it for a long moment and then he began to smile. It was a full-bodied, satisfied smile—the smile of a man whose hand has been called when he's holding a royal flush.

TICKET TO $25,000

The silence in the den was sudden and absolute.

Major Wiley, his eyes gleaming with excitement, held up the bankbook so Colonel Griswold could see it.

"We've got him, sir. By God, we've got him. You wouldn't think they'd be so stupid, but time after time we find the evidence. And this is it."

The colonel reached out, but the major held it back. "Sir, let Mcintosh get you some gloves."

And in an instant the big sergeant had the gloves and the colonel was pulling them on, his face closed and unreadable.

Mother tried to push past the sergeant. "Let me see it," she demanded. "Let me by. This is ridiculous. That's just our bankbook. What do you mean 'it's proof'?"

Colonel Griswold was looking at the bankbook now. His face hardened. The shaggy air of embarrassment was gone. He looked at my mother and she drew back. He no longer looked with the face of a friend.

"Is this your bankbook?" he asked, his voice sharp and demanding.

Mother sensed the danger, too. Her face was still and her voice wary. "It looks like it, but I can't tell from here."

Colonel Griswold held it up so that the name showed, black print against a blue cover: The Traders' National Savings and Loan Association.

Mother hesitated, then said, "The Traders' National Savings and Loan is where we keep our account."

"One account?" the colonel asked.

"Yes, of course," she said quickly. "We have one account with about seven thousand dollars in it."

"This is a different account," Colonel Griswold said grimly. "It's in the name of Mitchell Harmon and it shows one deposit of twenty-five thousand dollars."

"It's certainly not ours," Mother said in quick relief. "We only have one account and Mike isn't anybody named Mitchell Harmon."

"Look at it, Celia," the colonel said tiredly, and he held out the booklet for her to see the signature of Mitchell Harmon.

Her face thinned.

Colonel Griswold nodded. "That's right. It's Mike's handwriting, isn't it? I know it and you know it."

"It's a forgery," she said immediately. And I was proud of her. Her voice didn't waver and her clear-green eyes looked full at the colonel.

"That will be for the defense to prove," Colonel Griswold replied, and there was nothing left in his voice now—not anger, not sorrow, not anything.

"Bill!" Mother grabbed his arm. "Bill, you can't believe this about Mike! He loves the Army. It's his life. He wouldn't sell out his country for twenty-five *million* dollars."

The colonel made no reply. He handed the bankbook to the major, who carefully tucked it in an attaché case.

"Continue to search, Major."

Then the colonel leaned over and picked up the telephone receiver and dialed.

"Colonel Griswold here. Colonel Hastings is to be detained pending further investigation. Notify General Loring that the search has yielded evidence and that I will call him with a full report when the search is completed. Inform Colonel Hastings that he has a right to counsel and that anything he says may be used against him."

The colonel listened for a moment, then said, "Right. If that's the general's wish, I will meet with him as soon as we finish here."

His call finished, the colonel stayed right with the searchers. The search was expert and thorough. It lasted two more hours and it covered our quarters from the basement to the attic.

And it didn't turn up anything else at all.

When it was done, Mother watched the men boxing up all of Dad's private correspondence to take along for further study, and she tried one more time.

"Bill, can't you see that this is a plant? The only thing you found was that bankbook, and no one but a fool would hide something like that in such an obvious fashion. Mike is neither a traitor nor a fool. After all, it was he who suggested that you search the quarters."

"Sometimes a man can be overconfident," the colonel said obliquely.

Mother sighed. "I thought you were Mike's friend. You were at the Point together. How can you believe it? Why would he do something like this? Money has never meant anything to him."

Colonel Griswold emptied into a carton the contents of the tin box in which Dad kept his checkbook stubs and canceled checks, then he looked at my mother.

"This kind of thing happens," he said dully. "The Swedes

trusted Colonel Wennerstrom, too, and he was a Soviet agent for years. Maybe Mike turned against the war when Kyle was killed." He looked over at me. "Look at Bart. A peace marcher. You learn those kind of attitudes at home, don't you?"

But Mother turned away when he mentioned Kyle. I don't know if she even heard that crack about me. She walked blindly into the living room.

"So my dad's a traitor because I walked in a peace march?" I said angrily. "That's guilt by association, isn't it? That's the right-wing America First credo, isn't it? Anybody's a Communist who doesn't want to fight in lousy little wars in lousy little countries to keep America First. So that makes my dad a Communist?"

"I don't know what your father is," the colonel replied evenly. "It looks like he's a traitor. But I know what you are. You're a smart punk. Left wing, right wing, those are just words. I'm an Army officer trying to do his job. I didn't say your father was a Communist because you are a marshmallow punk. The evidence shows he's a traitor. The weapon is gone and there's a ticket to twenty-five thousand dollars stuck under his desk. What does it look like to you?"

"A frame."

Colonel Griswold shrugged. "A frame by whom? The Army? The Army can make a lot of mistakes, but, buddy, it doesn't frame people."

"By whomever stole the gun!"

"Yeah," the colonel said heavily. "Maybe somebody sprinkled the M-18 with invisible ink and waltzed out with it. That's the only other way it could've gone."

I started to ask the colonel what exactly had happened or what the CID thought had happened, but he was through with me. He was mad at me and my dad and the whole world. It must be tough to find evidence that your best friend was a traitor. I could almost understand how it could kick you. What I couldn't understand was how anybody could believe it of my dad.

In another ten minutes everything was boxed up and ready to go, and Colonel Griswold was barking orders like a drill sergeant. Then, abruptly, they were gone and the house was as quiet as a church at midnight.

The house looked frowsy and that was all wrong. My mother didn't keep a frowsy house. Scraps of paper spotted the hall. The Oriental throw rug was askew. In the living room and dining room the furniture was all a little out of place.

I bent down and straightened the throw rug, then I started picking up the litter that had straggled over the hall during the search. I was almost finished putting everything back in place in the dining room when Mother called me.

"Bart, come here, please."

I pushed the hutch back even with the wall then crossed to the living room. She was at Dad's desk in the den. I paused in the doorway. "What are you doing, Mom?"

She tapped her pencil on a sheet of paper on the desk top. "I'm trying to make some sense out of all this. First I tried to call Colonel Antonelli."

"Who?"

"You know, Bart, he's the staff judge-advocate. But when I dialed, a voice came on the line and said all calls from these quarters had to be approved by Colonel Griswold. I said not to bother."

I slammed my hand against the doorframe. "The pigs! Who do they think they are? That's outrageous! The whole thing's insane. Acting like Dad is some Communist spy!"

"Bart, listen to me!" Mother said sharply.

"Well, isn't it crazy?" I demanded. "It's the old Red Threat rearing its ugly head. Somebody probably just lost the damned gun."

"Oh, Bart, you fool! No one 'lost' that bankbook. It was put there deliberately. It's either a Communist conspiracy—or your father's guilty!"

Some shocks you can't absorb. The whole evening, coming right on the heels of the screaming mob in town, had seemed unreal. The CID in our quarters. My dad detained in the stockade. It was like one of those mod movies where one scene glides into another, a street cleaner in the gutter on the bottom of the screen and a girl in a bikini stretched out on the top of the screen.

All along I had clung tightly to the belief that it was one of those wild, stupid, freakish mistakes that the Army can make sometimes, like sending all the gear for a scuba outfit to a desert outpost.

"But it has to be a mistake," I said weakly. "It has to be!"

"The Army doesn't make mistakes about top secret weapons, Bart. And you are talking about your father's command. Do you think he could make that kind of mistake?"

"But we don't know what happened," I insisted. "It could be a mistake."

"So it's a mistake," Mother said bitingly. "You'd rather believe your father negligent in his command than believe in Communist agents. Oh Bart, don't you see, the gun has been stolen and who else would steal it? And where else did that bankbook come from?"

I walked over and slumped into the wicker chair next to the fireplace. She was right. I didn't believe Communist agents were under every bed. And I didn't believe there were spies and collaborators strewn throughout the country, despite the forebodings of the House Un-American Activities Committee.

Mother paused then said gently, "Look, Bart, facing the fact of international espionage doesn't mean you blame any and every bad thing that happens on the Communist bogeyman. But you'd better believe there is at least one, and perhaps more, Soviet agents assigned to Fort Calhoun."

I suppose I still looked unconvinced.

She shook her head. "You just don't know very much. Does the name Rudolph Able mean anything to you?"

I frowned. "Wasn't he convicted of something?"

She sighed at that. "Yes. Espionage. He posed as an American citizen in New York, but he was really a colonel in the KGB, the Russian equivalent to our CIA. Colonel Able headed a wide network of Soviet spies."

"So you really think there is a Soviet agent in residence here?" I asked slowly.

Mother shrugged. "Take your pick, Bart. A Soviet agent or your father."

I pushed up out of my chair and wandered aimlessly around the den. I paused in front of the fireplace and looked up at the portrait of my grandfather, General Barton McDonald Hastings. I was named for him. In World War II his men called him "Black Bart." He was in the Pacific Theater, and they said the frown didn't leave his face until our troops landed in Japan.

People say I look like him. The portrait was painted when he was one of the Army's youngest generals. His hair was black as pitch and sleeked back from a high forehead. His chin was square and his eyes as black and hard as lumps of coal. Black Bart had been a tough man. He'd been on an aerial survey of his troops in Korea when his sleet-laden plane slammed into the side of a hill.

I swung around and faced Mother. "Look, Mom, it could be a snafu—but we can't do anything until we know what happened! We've got to find out what happened!"

"We're stymied, Bart. That's why I tried to call Colonel

Antonelli. The CID is sure to have briefed the Judge Advocate General's office because JAG will provide counsel both for the prosecution and the defense."

"The JAG office! Of course! I'll talk to Captain Andy."

"Captain Andy?"

"You know, Mom, Captain Brainard. He was scoutmaster when I made Eagle Scout. He's in JAG. I'll bet I can find out from him." And I started for the door.

"Wait, son. You'd better change your clothes."

"Oh, Mother! I'm not going to a social."

"I know that, but torn and dirty clothes are a little noticeable on post and it might be as well if no one saw you with Captain Brainard."

"Why not?"

"For his sake."

"What are you trying to say?" I asked slowly.

Mother looked up at me tiredly. Her face was pale and the dark smudges under her eyes emphasized the fragility of her narrow heart-shaped face. She said reluctantly, "You must understand, Bart, if the captain won't talk to you."

"But Captain Andy's a great guy. He's first rate, Mother."

"JAG officers aren't supposed to discuss cases in which they may become involved. And he has his career to consider."

"I know he'll help," I said stubbornly. "Captain Andy's okay."

"You can try," she said.

I went upstairs on the double. In the old-fashioned bathroom, with its white tub that stood on claw legs, I bent close to the mirror and carefully washed away the blood and dirt from the side of my head. It wasn't a big deal, though. The blood had come from a broad scratch and the bump wasn't bad. Unless you looked close, it was my ordinary face. In my room, I switched to a clean shirt and slacks and I was ready to go.

When I started down the stairs, jingling my key ring in my hand, I was almost cheerful. Captain Andy would tell me what had happened and we could start untangling the whole mess.

I slammed out the front door and thudded across the wooden porch to the steps.

The beam of the flashlight caught me full in the face and I stumbled a little on the steps.

"Halt! Who goes there?" a voice demanded sharply.

I threw up my hand to shade my eyes. In the softly spreading light from the wrought iron lamppost at the curb, I could see the freshly-starched khakis and the white armband and the sergeant's patches on his sleeves.

An MP sergeant.

"Identification, please."

The flashlight beam didn't waver from my face. I could see the solid stance of his feet, ankles encased in stiff, white webbing, and the white-gloved hand clamped to the butt of the gun holstered on his right hip.

I had been absent from an Army post for a full school year, but the reflexes of an Army brat are deep-buried and automatic. I reached into my hip pocket, pulled out my billfold, and handed it to him.

His right hand left the gun butt to take the billfold. He flipped it open and swung the flashlight down on the ID card, then flashed the light full in my face again.

"Mr. Hastings, you are requested to remain in your father's quarters tonight."

"And if I don't?" I asked levelly.

"I will be forced to take you into custody and proceed to the stockade."

He handed back the billfold. I took it and turned and walked back up the steps and into the house.

CROSSING THE POST

It didn't take a minute to change clothes again. This time I pulled on Levi's and sneakers and a dark-blue polo shirt. Mother stood in the open door of my room with a worried frown on her face.

"Do you really think you should, Bart?"

"What're the odds?" I asked. "I might as well be officially barred from the post as sitting here in the house twiddling my thumbs. I can't help Dad either way, but I'd rather be counted out on the mat than lose it on points."

She nodded slowly and stepped out of my way. I headed up the narrow flight of stairs that led to the attic.

As I opened the attic door, she called, "Be careful, Bart." I waved my hand, then pulled the door shut behind me. I paused for a minute, until my eyes adjusted to the dark. Darker shadows slowly took shape. To my left were a couple of foot-lockers that held odds and ends picked up in years of knocking about the world. Close to my feet was a newer footlocker. I didn't need any light to know the name stenciled on it. It had belonged to Lieutenant Kyle Alan Hastings. And now it had the dust of a year on it.

A soft glimmer of light at the back end of the attic marked a dormer window. I walked to it, skirting the footlockers, an old chest of drawers, and a stack of storage crates.

Since it was an unfinished attic, the window wasn't screened. I gave it a push and it slid smoothly up. Trust the dormer windows in Army quarters to slick right up. Probably some maintenance man had oiled them the last time the roof was shingled.

Living on an Army post can have its drawbacks. At its worst, it can be as smothering as the close little world of a New England village. But there are some pluses. If the fuses don't work, call the maintenance men. If a doorknob breaks, call the maintenance men. The Army frowns on do-it-yourself improvements. Houses are painted on a regular schedule, and tough on you if you don't want it done right then.

But I was grateful to the ubiquitous maintenance men when that window slid up easy as you please. I couldn't afford a squeak or a rattle. If an MP doesn't hear like a cat, he's darn well expected to.

The thick, massive branches of an old oak tree masked the window from view of the ground. I stepped out on a branch and slowly moved to the center of the tree, and then I pressed against the bole and looked through the shifting wind-stirred leaves toward the ground—and I spotted the second MP.

He was standing about five feet from the back porch, big as life and twice as obvious. They certainly hadn't picked him for his subtlety. I smiled for the first time in hours and, on the side of the tree opposite him, began to ooze down as quietly as a boa constrictor after a white rat.

I dropped the last ten feet to the ground and ducked behind a honeysuckle bush. About thirty feet back our yard dropped off into a ravine. On the other side of the ravine rose a thickly-wooded hill and, on its far slope, were more senior officers' quarters.

I waited for a minute behind the honeysuckle bush, but no

voice was raised in alarm. I moved down the yard, darting quickly from one tree to another until I reached the ravine and the skinny little path that dropped down the slope.

The path wasn't a direct route to anywhere but I knew it eventually led down to some stepping stones that crossed the stream and then up the hillside to the dirt road that topped the rise.

It was dark enough in those woods to satisfy any witch planning a midnight Black Mass. I picked my way along the path, feeling my way with my feet.

And all the while I wanted to run. I wanted to get to Captain Andy. He would know what had happened. And hearing him talk, maybe I'd figure out some way to help Dad.

I kept my patience all the way to the stream. There wasn't much water. It was just a blackish murmur in the night. I hopped on the stones, one-two-three, and I was across. Then I ran out of patience.

I struck out blindly up the slope. It took me less than a minute to regain the path. A straight line may be the shortest distance between two points but the dry underbrush and crackling mounds of old leaves made enough noise to bring out either the MPs or the rattlesnakes, so I started my soft-shoe up the winding path again.

It seemed an age, but I guess it didn't take more than fifteen minutes to follow the path to the top of the hill, cross the dirt road, and plunge down the other side. The path meandered along behind officers' quarters then finally ended at the grassy edge of a baseball diamond.

To the left I could see the double lanes of Pershing Avenue, the main artery into the post. A car swept up Pershing and I almost ducked, but there wasn't any need. I was on the far side of the diamond and somebody would have to be looking to notice me.

I crossed the baseball diamond and walked briskly up the sidewalk on a street that led to the center of the post. Lights showed in some of the old houses. I could hear music and sometimes people laughing and once the tinny notes of an old-time player piano. Life was going on as it does every Friday night on Army posts all over the world—for everybody except my dad.

It made me mad. I could just hear it. Probably in that house there—that old two-story one—with a bunch of cars parked out in front, some lieutenant colonel on his second brandy was pausing while he lit his cigar and asking cautiously, "Have you heard about Colonel Hastings?"

So I wasn't paying any attention to occasional cars. I was all wrapped up in my thoughts and walking as fast as I could. And if there's anybody out of place on a quiet street on an Army post at midnight, it's a man in a tearing hurry.

The spotlight hit me full in the face. I stopped, threw up my arm, and turned instinctively to run.

"Halt. Halt!"

And two MPs jumped out of their car and started running up the sidewalk.

I stopped short and got down on my knees and pawed in the bushes lining the sidewalk.

"Here, Sebastian. Here, kitty, kitty. Come here, you devil."

I wormed a little farther into the shrubbery. I could hear the MPs. They were still coming, but they weren't running and they weren't yelling "Halt!"

I called again, a little louder. "Come on, Sebastian. Nice kitty. Pretty kitty. Come here, you rat fink."

The footsteps were right behind me now and one of the MPs was snickering.

"Hey, buddy," one of them called. "Lost something?"

I backed out of the shrubbery and stood up to face them.

"Why anybody wants to keep cats, I don't know," I growled. "And if some morning Mother finds that stupid Siamese with his throat cut, you'll know who did it."

The bigger MP flashed his light this way and that in the shrubbery.

"I don't see him anywhere," he said slowly.

"The light," I replied tiredly. "That's how I lost him again. When you guys flashed your light at me, Sebastian took off." I turned back toward the shrubbery and called, "Here, kitty. Come on, Sebastian. Nice kitty."

"Where do you live, kid?"

I jerked my thumb over my shoulder. "Colonel McLemore's quarters."

"Got your ID?" he asked.

Cat or no cat, this guy wasn't anybody's fool. I reached for my hip pocket, then shrugged. "Sorry. I was getting ready for bed when Mother asked me to put her car up and that's when Sebastian got out. I can run in and get it."

The big MP shrugged. "Oh, I guess it's all right. You go on and find your cat."

"Thanks. I will unless he's found a tabby first."

The MPs laughed and one of them said, "There's always that, huh, kid? Well, happy hunting."

I started fooling around in the bushes, calling my imaginary Sebastian. I waited until the patrol car had moved on and turned the corner. Then I cut swiftly up the McLemore's drive. It was going to be a backyard-and-alley jaunt from this point on. There just aren't any pedestrians that late on a post and I doubted I could get away with Sebastian again.

This was the oldest part of the post and dirt alleys ran behind the houses. McLemore's alley was my goal. Unless some colonel was fooling around in his garage after midnight, I shouldn't run into anybody.

And I didn't. A couple of dogs barked pretty loud when I passed, but I didn't linger long enough by anybody's fence to really get a row started.

So I reached Taylor Boulevard, which backs on Pershing Oval. The layout of the post was really pretty simple. Pershing was the main road into the post. It swept along past barracks, the NCO club, and closer in, Logan Memorial Hospital. Then it started a big curve and there were the commissary and the post exchange. By the time it passed the PX, Pershing was running due east. It looped around near the river then turned back and ran into itself. The loop formed a big oval which was the heart of the post—the post headquarters, the brigade headquarters, provost marshal's office, judge advocate general's office, the battalion headquarters.

Taylor, where I stood, ran east and west. To my left—east—it crossed Pershing. Beyond it to the north lay the oval. And, baby, was that ever patrolled. In addition to the street patrols, MPs hourly checked each and every building to be sure they were secured.

Somehow or other I had to cross that whole area because the bachelor officers' quarters lay a block beyond the oval in an old wooden group of row houses on Washington Boulevard.

I finally decided to circle to my left and try to reach the BOQ from the rear. It meant crossing Pershing, but I had to cross it somewhere and anything was better than trying to move near the oval.

It took me twenty minutes to reach the BOQ and I was really wrung out. I crossed Pershing when it lay quiet and empty, the street lights spreading like spots on an empty stage. I circled around through the hospital grounds and behind the commissary and PX and up the alley behind the enlisted men's mess, and then I was in the shadow of the iron fire-escape behind the BOQ.

I was halfway up the fire escape when I heard a car turning into the alley. I went up those metal steps faster than a lieutenant salutes a general. I yanked open the screen door and hurtled into the hall and stood there panting as headlights flashed up the alley.

I'd made it. But I didn't hurry to Captain Andy's door. I waited until the sweat dried on my face and my breathing had evened out.

I had to be on top of it to talk to Captain Andy.

THEFT AT BLUE BOWL

For a long sickening minute I didn't think Captain Andy was going to let me in. He opened the door at my second knock and then he just stood there, his big, stocky body blocking the doorway. I couldn't see his face very well in the dim light of the hall. He stood there, his face in the shadow, and said nothing at all.

"Captain Andy, I've got to talk to you."

His big shoulders slouched as if he were very tired, the kind of a slouch a lineman gives when the game is over and his team has lost. Slowly he stepped back into the room and held the door for me to come in.

I walked uncertainly to the center of the room and stopped. It was the living room of a small apartment. The furnishings were quartermaster stuff: a green slip-covered divan, a tan slip-covered easy chair, some glass-paned bookcases, and a desk. The only personal note was a painting over the gray stone fireplace, the vivid splash of color of a city at night.

Captain Andy moved heavily past me and walked into the kitchenette.

"Something to drink, Bart? I've got Cokes."

"A Coke'll be fine, sir."

I was still standing in the middle of the room when he came back with a beer in one hand and a Coke in the other. He handed me the Coke and gestured toward the couch. "Sit down, Bart."

I sat down and drank some of the Coke and waited.

He sank into the big overstuffed easy chair, and suddenly it looked small. He's a big man, about six foot three, and everything about him is big—great ham-like hands, broad heavy shoulders, a massive head with a thick mane of blond hair.

He drank half his beer in one great swallow, then looked across the room at me. "I thought you and your mother were confined to quarters."

"We are. But I had to see you, Captain Andy. Mother and I don't know what's going on, what happened. I know it must be some kind of gigantic mistake but—"

The slow shake of that massive head stopped me cold. I stood up and I was shaking all over.

"Captain Andy, you don't believe it, do you? Not about my dad! You can't!"

"Sit down, Bart. The Army doesn't make that kind of mistake—"

I started blindly for the door, but he lunged up from his chair and one of those great hands caught me by the shoulder.

"Sit down, boy."

I walked stiffly back to the couch. All night I'd held onto the fragile hope that it was a great big snafu.

"I didn't say your dad was guilty. But there's no mistake about the weapon being stolen. It's really simple, Bart; either your father's a traitor or he's been framed."

Captain Andy finished his beer, then sat down beside me. "I've prosecuted and defended at a lot of courts-martial, Bart. The Army doesn't bring charges unless it's a sure thing. A real sure thing. I think I've only defended one innocent man in the whole time I've been in the JAG Corps. That doesn't mean I lost all the cases I defended. I've won quite a few. It doesn't matter to defense counsel whether a man is innocent or guilty. That's for the court to decide. A man is entitled to an honest defense if he's as black-hearted and guilty as the devil."

I looked up at Captain Andy and he could see the bewilderment in my eyes.

"You don't see what my won-lost record has to do with the price of peanuts? Just this, Bart. I've become pretty good at judging whether a man's telling the truth. And against all the evidence, I believe your dad when he says he didn't do it."

I'm surprised my grin didn't split my face open. Those were the sweetest words I'd heard in a long time. Then, slowly, the grin slipped off my face, because Captain Andy was shaking his big head again.

"What I think about your dad doesn't have anything to do with the price of peanuts, either. I'm only telling you what I think as a man. Because there isn't a thing in the world I can do to help you."

"What d' you mean?" I asked slowly.

"I'm just a hired hand. And Colonel Antonelli has assigned me to assist the investigating officer at the Article 32 and to generally keep on top of the investigation."

"Article 32?"

"That's the Army's equivalent to a preliminary hearing," he explained. "When a serious crime is committed, the commanding general appoints an investigating officer to hold an Article 32 investigation. Testimony is taken and the investigating officer reports to the general whether there are grounds for a court-martial. The commanding general evaluates the report, and if the facts warrant it, he orders the court-martial."

"Has an Article 32 been scheduled?"

"For 0900, Monday, in the JAG courtroom. Colonel Krueger's been named investigating officer. He will conduct the Article 32, questioning all the witnesses. He will have at hand the CID report and the sworn statements. That same material will have been furnished to the defense counsel. Captain Brody has been appointed to represent your dad at the Article 32. He has the right to cross-examine all the witnesses. When the testimony is completed, Colonel Krueger will make his report to General Loring."

"And you'll be on hand to help Colonel Krueger?"

He nodded. "If he has any questions of procedure, that sort of thing. Although, really, an Article 32 is pretty loose. He can run it any way he wants to. First, he'll probably call on the CID to present the evidence against the accused."

The evidence against the accused. The evidence against my father.

"And what is the case against the accused?" I asked, my voice thick in my throat.

Captain Andy got up from the couch and paced across the room, then turned to face me. His iron-gray eyes looked somberly at me, then fastened on the floor.

"It's against Army regs for a JAG officer to discuss his cases." He paused and said quietly, "I'm on the list for promotion to major. It should come through in a couple of months—if nothing happens to queer it. Like leaking information on an espionage case."

Then he laughed. A short, grim laugh. "But my father always said rules were made to be broken. Did you ever hear of General Brainard? He disobeyed orders in the field one time. But they never had a board of inquiry. He won the battle. His troops would've been slaughtered if he'd followed the battle plan."

"I won't let anyone know you talked to me, Captain Andy. I promise you that."

He walked back to the overstuffed chair and sank heavily into it. "It's been a hell of a night. The CID called us into it when they found the passbook taped under your dad's desk. In their view, that clinched it because all the other evidence pointed to your dad, anyway."

"What evidence?"

"It starts with the arrival of the M-18s Tuesday morning," he began slowly. "I'm sure you've heard the skinny on post about the new M-18. This is the first time out from under wraps. There's been only limited production. A couple of thousand, I think, but that's classified. Anyway, it's our newest, latest rifle, and the factory sent the first shipment here to Fort Calhoun to be tested in the field. And that's where your dad enters the picture. He a brigade commander, of course, but he's such a first-rate infantryman that the Pentagon asked him to pick a company from one of the brigade battalions and to personally supervise a real rugged test for the M-18. The actual field testing is supposed to begin next Monday, but I don't know what will happen now. Probably be put off a couple of weeks."

I rubbed my hand against the linen cover of the couch. Yeah, they'd have to put it off, because Colonel Hastings was going to be tied up in court.

Captain Andy rubbed his face. "But that's for the Pentagon to worry about. Anyway, the shipment of M-18s arrived on the post Tuesday morning in a guarded cargo plane. Your father was at the airfield when the shipment came in, with a special detail from Transportation. They transferred the weapons to a specially prepared arms room at a training camp in the Blue Bowl sector. Do you know where I mean?"

I nodded impatiently. On a big troop post, the Army names the various training sectors. Blue Bowl was a tract of rugged country about five miles from the main post. Blue Bowl covered about sixty acres of heavily wooded, ravine-laced land and was used only for very special training purposes.

"So they got the rifles to Blue Bowl. Then what happened?"

"They took the crates into the arms room. It's in the basement of an old farmhouse that serves as command post for Blue Bowl. Do you know how an arms room is set up? The rifles are stacked in gun racks, thirty rifles to a rack, ten racks in all. They stacked the rifles, padlocked the racks, then secured the arms room. So all three hundred rifles were in place Tuesday afternoon. Your dad confirms it. The Transportation captain confirms it. The sergeant in charge of the arms room confirms it."

"When was the rifle taken?"

"Apparently on Wednesday morning," he said. "But I'll get back to that in a minute," He got up and crossed to the desk, pulled a legal pad out of a drawer, and picked up a ballpoint.

"Come here, Bart. Let me sketch it for you. You've got to get the picture about the command post."

And all the while he was talking, Captain Andy's broad hand moved, marking out the square of a farmhouse, drawing a high fence, shading around it to show thick woods.

"This is an old farmhouse. It sits on Whaleback Ridge and it's about three miles from the nearest blacktop. The only road to it is a winding dirt lane. There are four checkpoints set up on that dirt road. Anybody coming up that road has to stop and show his pass to the sentries. Have you got that?"

"Yeah."

"Okay, so you see what kind of security your dad had going?"

I nodded.

"Then you come to the command post itself. It's surrounded by a five-strand barbed-wire fence. There is one gate. It is manned at all times and nobody gets in without a special pass.

At night there are two men who circle the fence and each has his pal along, a German shepherd."

I began to get the picture, all right. And I began to feel sick. It hadn't been a slip-up. The kind of operation Captain Andy was describing didn't have slip-ups.

"What happened?" I demanded.

"The rifles were locked into the racks and the arms room secured at 1600 hours on Tuesday. On Wednesday the sergeant in charge of the arms room, Sfc. Timothy Sanders unlocked the door to the arms room at 0800 hours. He went in, turned on the lights, and found a note at the cage."

"Cage?"

"Like a ticket window but bigger," Captain Andy explained. "It blocks entrance to the arms room proper. Next Monday, when the exercise was scheduled to begin, the men from Company B would have lined up at the cage and each would have given his name, rank, serial number, and the number of his weapon. Sergeant Sanders would have yelled the weapon number, and a private would have hustled the M-18 up there, and the sergeant would have handed it over."

"So Sergeant Sanders found a note at the cage?"

"Yes. It was a note to Sanders informing him that the colonel had arrived early, had taken rifle number one, and would return it later in the day.

"Sergeant Sanders didn't question it until Wednesday afternoon, when it was time to secure the arms room. The sergeant didn't think he should close up without the rifle, so he called upstairs to the lieutenant. The lieutenant asked the captain. The captain dumped it in Major Kelly's lap. And the major didn't know what to think. He'd been with the colonel off and on all morning and the colonel hadn't mentioned the rifle. And the colonel had left at noon like he always did on Wednesday for physical training. Anyway, the major called your dad at the skeet range and, in effect, your dad said, 'What rifle? What note?' and the lid blew off."

I slammed my hand down on his desk and the legal pad slithered on the slick top. "But it's so obvious!" I said angrily. "Somebody forged that note and took the rifle."

Captain Andy carefully squared the legal pad in the center of the desk top. "That's what everybody assumed—at first. That's why your dad was just questioned all day Thursday and Friday and not immediately charged. But the more the evidence piled up, the clearer it became, at least to the CID, that your dad had written the note."

"That's stupid! Nobody incriminates himself."

"Not unless he thinks he can get away with it," Captain Andy replied. "The CID figures the note is a double bluff. Your dad can claim it was written to frame him, but the CID thinks he had to write it to be able to steal the rifle."

"Why?" I demanded.

"If the weapon had been gone when Sergeant Sanders opened the arms room at 0800 Wednesday and there had been no note from your father, what would have happened?" Captain Andy asked.

"The sergeant would have alerted Dad and the search for the M-18 would have started right then," I said cautiously.

"Right. But the note was there. So no alert was raised until late afternoon. And this, according to the CID, made it possible for your dad to smuggle the weapon out of the command post."

I shook my head. "That's what I can't understand! Why pitch it on my dad? Out of all the men in the command post, why say he's the one who smuggled it out? Just because of that stupid note? Why, it could've been anybody. It could—"

Capt. Andy held up his hand. "Not just anybody, Bart." As

he spoke, he flicked a finger down for each point. "Nobody but authorized personnel came into HQ compound either on Tuesday afternoon or Wednesday morning. The lock to the arms room hadn't been jimmied; so somebody used a key. Your dad had a key."

I started to interrupt, but he continued without pause, "The note, the necessary note to forestall search for the weapon, was written in your father's handwriting—or it's a gilt-edged forgery. The note is on your father's stationery. It even has some of his fingerprints on it."

Then Captain Andy looked straight at me. He snapped his thumb down and the whole fist was balled. "And there's the most damning point of all, the real clincher—only one man left the command post Wednesday carrying anything that could hold a rifle. That man was your father."

I licked my lips. "What was he carrying."

"A gun case."

ONE OF THEM'S A TRAITOR

The gun case. That's why Major Wiley had felt so sure. The gun case was the clincher. How could we ever prove Dad hadn't carried the missing M-18 out in his gun case?

Slowly I gathered up the yellow legal sheets that Captain Andy had written on, his sketch of the Blue Bowl command post, and the names of the men who had been in Blue Bowl on Wednesday morning. I folded the sheets and stuck them in my pocket.

Then I looked up at Captain Andy. "I can see how it looks, but I know Dad didn't take that rifle. And I want you to know that I really appreciate how you've leveled with me, because you can't get anywhere if you don't know where you are."

"I hope you get where you want to go, Bart," he said quietly. And it meant a lot because I knew he really did hope for me.

"Thanks, Captain Andy." I turned to go but he called out, "Hold it. I'll drive you home."

I swung around. "You can't! What if the MPs should stop you and find me in your car?"

"The MPs won't stop me," he said confidently. "And if you try to cross the post again on foot, your chances are lousy."

I started to object; I didn't want to put him in any kind of jeopardy, but he just gave me a shove between the shoulders and we were out the door.

And he was right on the money. We passed an MP car and the driver waved hello to Captain Andy, but nobody stopped us. And when we turned into the older residential area, we didn't even see any cars at all.

Captain Andy dropped me off at the dirt road that runs along the top of the wooded hill behind our quarters. Just enough moonlight slanted through the trees to show me the way. I took my time. The need for hurry was past and it would be hard to take if the MPs caught me out of quarters when I was so close to home.

When I slipped quietly up the path to our back yard, I saw the MP by the kitchen steps. He didn't look like he'd moved a muscle since I left. I skirted the far side of the honeysuckle bushes and made it back to the old oak tree. I pulled myself up in the tree and climbed back into the attic.

Once in my room, I sat on the edge of my bed and studied the yellow legal sheets I'd brought from Captain Andy's. I read the list of names over and over, then I shook my head. I couldn't do Dad any good by sitting in a stupor reading a list of names. I needed to get some sleep and start out fresh in the morning.

I pulled on my pajamas, turned off the light, and stretched out on my bed. I was asleep before I could pull up the sheet.

The thud of the morning paper against the front screen woke me. Maybe, subconsciously, I'd been listening for that familiar sound. I rolled out of bed and grabbed my robe and the yellow legal sheets and hurried into the hall.

Downstairs, I took a deep breath and stepped out onto the porch. A fresh MP stood watch at the bottom of the steps. I ignored him and picked up the paper. But I didn't open it.

Back in the hall, I hesitated a moment longer then abruptly

unfolded the paper. Whatever it was, we had to face it. Then, as my eyes scanned the page, I felt like a man who'd been handed a reprieve. It was the same old front page you read every day: a man shot down in a tavern, a list of local men killed in Vietnam, a heat-wave forecast, three killed in a car-truck crash on the Interstate, the city council calling for a new bond issue. But not a word about the theft of a classified weapon from Fort Calhoun.

Once I would have curled my lip, seeing the powerful hand of the Establishment muffing the news, keeping the facts from the people. But this time I was glad to see the secrecy clamped on. I knew Dad was innocent. I had a sudden empathy with people who see their names in print, accused of crimes. Accusation is enough for most readers.

I folded the paper and wondered sickly how long the general could keep the wraps on a story as big as this one. A full colonel accused of selling a classified weapon to the Russians. The papers would love it.

I walked on down the hall tiredly and pushed through the swinging door into the kitchen. Mother was at the breakfast table. In the clear morning sunlight, her hair shone even redder than usual. She looked up at me. Her face was pale, but two spots of color stained her cheeks.

"What's wrong?" I asked quickly. "Has something else happened?"

"Sit down, Bart, and I'll get you some breakfast," and she rose to get me a coffee cup and the plate of sweet rolls.

"Just some coffee, Mom. I'm not hungry. Tell me what's upset you."

"Nothing has happened. Absolutely nothing." She poured my coffee. "No one has called. No one has come. No one."

I drank deeply of the coffee and shrugged my shoulders. "So what?" I asked irritably. "Why should we want to see. . . ?"

And then I understood. My face flushed, too. "You mean Dad's already tried and convicted. You mean nobody has called. Not one of his friends."

"Not one."

"We've got one friend," I said quietly. "Captain Andy."

"He did talk to you then," Mother said, her voice lifting with hope.

"He talked to me." I reached across the table and patted Mother's arm. "It's grim. Really grim." I reached down into the pocket of my robe and pulled out a couple of crumped sheets from Captain Andy's legal pad.

"This is the set-up," I began, and I told her all of it, about the arms room and the patrols and the note and Dad's gun case.

She jumped on that at once.

"But he always carries his gun case on Wednesdays. That's PT afternoon. He goes skeet shooting every Wednesday. The gun case doesn't mean anything!"

I drank some more coffee. "It means one thing, Mother. It means trouble for Dad, because he was the only man who left the compound Wednesday carrying anything that could hold an M-18. They believe he brought the case in empty, got the M-18, broke it down, and put it in the case."

"They've just missed it somehow," Mother said angrily. "With all those men—"

She broke off as I shook my head.

"That's the kicker, Mom. It's not 'all those men.' Company B wasn't scheduled to bivouac until Monday so there were only the command officers and a skeleton crew. On Tuesday afternoon and Wednesday morning nine men had access to the command post."

I looked down at the second sheet of legal paper. Nine names listed in a row. And that was everybody who had set foot in the command post except for a maintenance man and two Signal Corps enlisted men who didn't count, because they'd been there on Tuesday morning and had left before the shipment arrived. Nine names all in a row.

Mother was reaching for the sheet when we heard the MP out front shout. By the time we got to the hall, the MP was halfway in the front door. Red-faced and angry, he stopped in the doorway and looked uncertain and a little scared,

"Miss, you can't come in here!" he remonstrated. "Nobody can. It's Colonel Griswold's orders!"

Nancy stood in the hall, her head thrown back, her smooth shining hair radiant in the sunlight that sparkled through the open door. Her dark-brown eyes flashed angrily.

"Go ahead and arrest me!" she ordered. "Pull me from the house!" She stood even straighter. "But I shall scream if you do."

"Miss, it's the colonel's orders!" And the anguish in his voice was heartfelt. He had his orders. But to forcibly drag the general's daughter out of the house! He flushed a little deeper and continued to stand in the doorway.

Mother put her hand on my arm. "Two friends," she said softly. And then she moved forward to Nancy.

"My dear, you'll never know what your coming means to Bart and me. But don't get embroiled in it. We'll—"

"Mrs. Hastings, I am in it and I won't leave." She paused and tears glittered in her eyes. "I don't believe it. I would as soon believe my father had stolen that rifle. It's insane." She looked back at the MP in the doorway. "And he's part of the nightmare."

The embarrassed, angry, and frustrated sergeant stepped back a pace from the blazing fury in her voice. Then Nancy's eyes focused on him. "Oh, sergeant, I don't mean you personally. It's not your fault. But to have MPs guarding these quarters!" She turned and caught my arm. "It isn't right, Bart, and I'm going to see about it this minute."

"But, Nancy, there isn't anything—" I shut up, because she already had the phone in her hand and she was hissing into the receiver, much as an angry kitten would face a dog.

"I don't care who gave what orders. This is Nancy Loring and I wish to speak to my father. Now! Immediately!"

The hall was abruptly electric with tension. I couldn't look at Mother. Nancy was with us. I knew suddenly and certainly that Nancy would always be with us. But I didn't know what Major General Martin Loring would say to his daughter. He was the commanding general and it would be he who would judge the investigating officer's report of the Article 32. I knew that his response to his daughter's call would mean more, a lot more, than whether MPs guarded us front and back.

And then she had him on the line.

"Daddy? I'm at Bart's house and I had to force my way in! Colonel Griswold has them absolutely shut off from the world. An MP in front and one in back and they can't use their telephone and all I have to say is, if that's the way you run an Army post then—"

She listened, then she replied quickly and decisively, "That's right. They are being treated like criminals and I don't care what kind of evidence the CID has gathered, it doesn't give them any right to—"

She paused for a long moment, then said gravely, "I know. I understand that, Daddy." She listened for a moment more, then swung around and gestured to the sergeant, "My father wants to talk to you."

I thought for a minute that the sergeant was going to dissolve right there in our doorway, but he made it to the phone. His "Yes, sir," was strong and clear, but his hand was shaking. He nodded once or twice into the receiver, then said, "Yes, sir. Right away, General Loring."

He put the phone down, took a deep breath and looked warily at Nancy. "The watch has been removed, miss. As of now." He backed away, then turned on his heel and was out the door in a flash.

"The sergeant meets the general's daughter," I said dryly.

Nancy flushed. "You make it sound horrid. You know I never do things like this."

I reached out and grabbed her hand. "I know that," I said quickly. "You're the most un-general general's daughter I've ever met." And I didn't try to be clever when I said softly, "And the most loyal friend I've ever had."

She looked steadily at me out of those magnificent black-brown eyes and there weren't any tears this time, just certainty. "I know it isn't true about your dad."

I hesitated, but I had to ask it. "Is it really all right with your dad—that you're here?"

"I'd be here whether or not it was all right with him. But he said he was glad I had come, that now was the time for friends to come." She sighed. "He said that I had to understand why he couldn't be here, too. But that he was the general and he had to do his duty."

She saw the despair on my mother's face.

"Mrs. Hastings, you know he admires the colonel!"

Mother nodded but she turned away and walked quickly down the hall toward the kitchen.

Nancy hurried after her. "Please, Mrs. Hastings. Daddy didn't know about the MPs. He was furious."

Mother turned to Nancy. After a moment, she said slowly, "I'm glad to know that, Nancy. And I appreciate your coming and—and eveything. But it's all so frightening. And we're so helpless!" Then her slight shoulders straightened and she forced a smile. "Come along to the kitchen. We'll have some coffee." She looked back up the hall at me. "Bart, you go up and dress. We'll wait for you in the kitchen."

"Hurry, Bart!" Nancy called. "We have to get busy. We've got to figure out what really happened."

It was almost like old times as I pounded up the stairs. I was happy. Nancy believed in us. And maybe we could do something. By golly, we would do something!

That surge of excitement and hope lasted all the way upstairs and back down again. I banged into the kitchen, ruffled Nancy's hair, then sat down beside her.

"Some coffee, please, Mom." I grinned at Nancy, then spread the legal sheets out on the table. "This is what's happened." But as I outlined it for her, as I listed all the damning points, my voice dulled. When I finished, I laid down the pencil I had brought downstairs with me. What was there to write?

"That's it," I said finally. "And I don't see a loophole. I don't see one."

Nancy shivered suddenly. "It's terrifying. So meticulously planned. It's brilliant, absolutely brilliant."

"What are you talking about?" I asked blankly.

She looked at me in surprise. "Don't you see it, Bart? Why, everybody should see it! This was no spur-of-the-moment thing, no pick-up-the-gun-and-run deal. This has been planned down to the last detail."

She hitched her chair closer to mine and reached for the yellow sheets. "Look at it. It's all been calculated to incriminate your father. The whole thing is pinned to the fact that he carries his gun case every Wednesday. That's the big thing. Then the note to Sergeant Sanders. It's like a chess move, with everything falling into place ten plays later. The note had to be forged with your dad's signature. If the thief had used anybody else's name, like Major Kelly's or Captain Tinsley's, why, Sergeant Sanders would have checked with them at once. But the note in your dad's handwriting makes it sure that no alarm is raised until late in the afternoon—*after* your dad has left the compound with his gun case."

"And the trap had sprung shut," I said thinly, and I felt cold all over. "And the CID, of course, sees it that Dad had to write the note, then claim it was a forgery. They don't see that only the note made it possible for the frame to be effective."

Nancy stared down at the yellow sheets. "I'll bet the thief picked your dad for the fall guy because of the gun case. Then, when he'd decided to hang it all on your dad, he got busy and found out where the colonel kept his savings account and started that new account, then hid the bankbook in your quarters. Oh, he really went after your dad."

Then I saw it, too. "You're right. It must have been planned well in advance." I grabbed the sheet with the nine names on it. "Maybe if we can find out which one knew the rifles were coming, we can spot our man."

Nancy frowned. "We can't hope for too much there, Bart. The leak on where and when the weapons were being shipped could have been at the factory or in Washington or somewhere else along the line. What we have to do is find out everything we can about the men on this list. There must be something that will give away the thief."

Nine names. Nancy and I bent close to the list.

Maj. Alfred Kelly
Capt. Carl Tinsley
Lt. Quentin Fagin
Sfc. Timothy Sanders

Sgt. Ed Royce
Sgt. Henry Krovich
Pfc. Lannie Elroy
Pfc. Diego Rodriguez
Pfc. William Schwartz

One of them was a traitor.

AT THE STOCKADE

I helped Mother pack Dad's kit bag, a fresh summer uniform, shoe polish, shorts, T-shirts, razor, shaving cream, toothbrush and paste. Mother stared down at the bag and its contents, and for a moment, she swayed on her feet. So many times she had packed for him. She had seen him off to World War II, to Korea, and to Vietnam. And now she packed for him because he was in the stockade.

"I know, Mom," I said quietly. "But we can't let it get us. Maybe when we talk to Dad, he'll remember something that will help."

She nodded and checked over the things in the bag. She hesitated for a minute, then crossed to the closet and pulled out his newest TWs, the slick worsted summer uniform, folded them and laid them gently in the bag. From the dresser she brought the case that held his decorations.

She didn't say anything but I understood. The TWs and the salad were for the Article 32. He was going to look every bit the soldier he was, Distinguished Service Cross and all. He'd won that one in Korea. His men had been pinned down by a machine-gun nest and Dad took it single-handed.

I carried the bag downstairs and held the car door for her.

We took her old Dodge but I drove. Mother sat still and small, holding the kit bag and staring blankly ahead.

I drove up Grant. The ground fell away to the right beyond the guard rail. Through the thick-leafed branches of the trees clinging to the cliffside, I would occasionally see fast-moving patches of brown muddy water. The river was swift and deep and wide along here.

We followed the river for six blocks and then we curved left, away from it. There on the hillside stood the commanding general's quarters. A gardener with hand clippers was trimming near a bricked walk. Even the grass stands at attention in a general's yard.

My hands clenched abruptly on the steering wheel and the car swerved a little, but I straightened it out immediately and Mother didn't seem to notice.

But the quick glimpse I'd had of General Loring and Nancy had hurt. They were dressed for tennis and the general was stowing the rackets in the back seat of his car. On their way to the officers' club, of course.

Nancy had left our house only about an hour before, when the call came that Mother and I could see Dad at three. Nancy and I had spent the day working on how to help Dad. And now she was going out to play tennis.

I tried to reason with myself. The world couldn't stop because the Hastings were in trouble. But it seemed all wrong. Everything seemed wrong. The bright, warm sunlight. The scent of honeysuckle, so thick you could smell it over a car's exhaust. The baby-blue sky with faint-white wisps of clouds.

It was a beautiful day—for everybody else.

And the oval was beautiful, too, the grass brilliantly green, the trees lush with leaves. Only an occasional pedestrian moved on the oval. The Army closes up shop at noon on Saturdays, except for the officer of the day, the staff duty officer, and the

MPs with weekend duty. Everyone else is free to relax, to play golf, to see a show, to shoot pool.

So I didn't have any trouble finding a parking place. I eased to a stop right in front of the provost marshal's. It was the second building on the oval and, like all but one, was of dingy-red brick with white stone steps leading up to double doors. The only exception was the new building at the end of the oval, Research and Development. It was a glass-and-white-brick job and it looked startlingly out of place among the dignified dowagers that had been there since the days when the post was young and cavalry horses had pounded up dirt roads.

At the top of the white steps, the double doors were propped open to let in any vagrant breeze, the provost marshal's office not running to air conditioning. Either the general hadn't seen fit to allocate any money for it or Colonel Griswold thought his MPs too tough for anything as soft as air conditioning.

But it wasn't hot inside. A couple of old-fashioned ceiling fans whirred high above, and the thick walls still held the cool of early morning. I wondered what the cells were like. The stockade was out in back of the office building.

As we crossed the yellow oak flooring to a waist-high counter, a brisk sergeant rose to greet us.

"Yes, ma'am," he said to my mother. "What can I do for you?"

"We have an appointment to see Colonel Hastings. I am Mrs. Hastings. Perhaps Colonel Griswold left word with you?"

His face was suddenly without any expression at all. He nodded. "Yes, ma'am, the colonel did. If you'll come this way, please." He held open a swinging gate at the end of the counter.

We followed him across the office and down a hall. All the doors on either side were shut. Nobody works on Saturday afternoon unless he has to. And why should the MPs or the CID work on the theft of the M-18? As far as they were concerned, it was solved.

At the end of the corridor, the sergeant opened a door that led out to a concrete walk covered by a breezeway. About fifteen yards ahead was the stockade.

It wasn't, of course, a stockade in the Old West sense. No wooden fence of saplings surrounded it. It was only a plain brick building, square and two story, but Mother faltered for a moment. The door was of iron and all the windows were barred.

Then she moved steadily on. The sergeant pushed in the heavy metal door and led us through an archway into a small, square room. Sunlight filtered through the small deep-set windows, throwing a slanted pattern of bars across the cement floor. Two straight-backed chairs sat on one side of a plain wooden table, a wicker divan on the other. The stippled plaster walls were painted gray.

"If you'll wait here, please, the colonel will be with you in a moment." He turned back through the archway. His heavy shoes stumped up the concrete hall. Then, unmistakably, metal clanged as a huge door opened and closed.

It seemed a long time that we waited there, but it was probably only a few minutes. Time seemed to stretch and swell in the deadened quiet of that thick-walled old building.

I wondered where they were keeping Dad. I'd never seen the cells in a stockade. Cells were a world apart from my life on an Army post. I'd been in a jail once, to visit a priest who'd been arrested for destroying Selective Service records.

His name was Father Conte. He had thick, unruly black hair, a narrow, intense face, and flashing black eyes—and he'd fought against the war in Vietnam with all the passion in his soul. I admired him. He was willing to go to jail, because he thought his country was wrong and he wasn't going to keep quiet about it.

And now I was in a jail again, to see another man I admired.

A man who loved his country and would follow its orders to a grave far from home without asking a question or counting the cost, because that was his duty.

And who was right and who was wrong?

The iron door clanged again, and Mother and I turned toward the archway.

Dad walked in, tall and lean, but I saw the difference a day could make. His khaki uniform was crumpled. His face was set and hard, angry and bewildered at the same time. The gleam of laughter, once so quick in his eyes that had dimmed when Kyle was killed, was gone completely.

Mother moved to meet him.

"Oh Mike, Mike darling!"

His arms closed around her and his head bent to hers and they held on to one another for a long moment.

I stood back and waited. This wasn't the time for me.

And then Dad looked up beyond Mother and when I saw the question in his eyes, I could have cried. I moved so fast I stumbled. His arm reached out to catch me in the bear hug he'd had for Kyle and me ever since we were little.

"I'm glad you came, Son." His voice was gruff and thick in his throat.

I held tight to his arm. "Of course I came, Dad. Listen, Daddy, it's going to be all right. Mother and I are working on it and it's going to be all right."

He looked at me out of dark-brown eyes, tired eyes, and there was a surge of warmth—but no hope. And I knew myself that my words sounded like the pledge you make to a child that everything is all right now, don't be frightened. And it's not all right, because the world is dark and dangerous and the tigers of the night prowl roundabout and there is no safety and no promise that anything will come right.

I took a deep breath and spaced my words. "It will be all right, Daddy. You see, we're ahead of the CID. We know you're innocent. And, like you've always said, every problem has an answer. We're going to find the answer."

Hope did flicker now in those tired eyes. He looked down at my mother and his face softened. "What are you and Bart up to, Celia?"

"We're going to find out who the traitor is," she said quietly. "We've got it narrowed down to nine men. Let Bart show you what he's worked out."

We sat on the wicker divan and pulled the table close. I spread open the yellow sheets of paper and laid it all out for Dad, everything I'd learned from Captain Andy and everything Nancy and I had surmised.

"So you see, it has to be one of the nine. Now, who would know that the shipment was coming?"

He looked at the list, then slowly shook his head. "Sooner or later, all of them. I first got word about setting up the exercise last month, about May fifth. It was no secret in the office. Major Kelly and I got started on planning the operation. Carl and Quentin were in on our talks, of course, to some extent. The whole thing would have sifted down to the rest of the men by the end of the week. It was a big topic of conversation."

I guess I looked pretty discouraged, because he clapped me on the shoulder and all his old vigor seemed back. "Don't worry, Bart. We'll beat this thing. I just needed to see you and your mother and get a fresh perspective. It all came as such a shock that it knocked me for a loop. But you're right, somebody did plan it. All we have to do is figure out who."

He studied the list of names, ticking a pencil against each one as if adding up a score in his mind.

"Mike, did the CID tell you anything at all about that

bankbook?" Mother asked suddenly. "The one they found hidden under the desk drawer."

Dad's lips thinned. "They've done practically nothing but shove that thing under my nose ever since last night."

I saw what Mother was after. "The date!" I exclaimed. "When was the account opened and the money put in it?"

"Of course!" Dad said quickly. Excitement surged in his voice. "The account was opened by mail on May twenty-first. The letter contained a check endorsed by Mitchell Harmon and instructions to open an account in his name. The letter's signature and the endorsement were faked to look like my writing."

He paused and shook his head. "It's a good forgery." He laughed with little humor. "If I didn't know better, I'd say I had signed it. Anyway, the letter gave a P.O. box number in Stockton for the bank's reply. The bank mailed a signature card on May twenty-sixth and received it back on May twenty-eighth. The bank then mailed the bankbook to the P.O. box on May thirtieth. It couldn't have gotten here before June second. And that was only last Monday!"

"That means the bankbook was hidden in our house this week," Mother said quickly. "On Monday or Tuesday or Wednesday! They'd have been sure to hide it before the rifle was stolen, so it was probably put there late on Monday or sometime Tuesday."

"That really gives us something to work on," Dad said eagerly. "Try the neighbors, Celia. See if you can get any trace of someone who didn't belong. No peddlers are permitted on post, of course, so a stranger may have been noticed."

"What if it wasn't a stranger?" I asked slowly.

His eyes darkened. "I know. We won't exclude anybody. Celia, make a list of everyone who came to the house." He frowned. "And when you have your list, hire a private detective in Stockton to see if he can pick up the least ambiguity about any of them."

"But, Dad," I objected, "all that will take forever and the Article 32 is scheduled for Monday."

He looked at me somberly. "They usually allow at least a month between an Article 32 and the court-martial."

"But I was hoping we could work hard and round up something to help before Monday," I said unhappily. "I was going to talk to all of the nine and see if something wouldn't turn up."

"That's an excellent plan, Bart, but that bankbook will decide the Article 32."

"The bankbook." I paused and then slowly I began to smile. "Dad, that passbook! It can't possibly have your fingerprints on it! That should throw the CID. Have your counsel ask about it at the 32 and let's see them explain that!"

Dad gripped my arm. "Bart, you're right! There's no way." His face seemed to reform. He looked ten years younger than the strained, tight-lipped man who had walked into this room an hour ago. He shook his head in wonder. "You know something? I'd almost given up until you and your mother came. It was so big and whichever way I turned I seemed to be trapped. But now, I feel like I have a chance—and that's all you ever need."

His face was relaxed and confident when he bent again to look at my list of nine names. The pencil checked Major Kelly. "He's been my exec for two years and he's a sound man. Not from the Point, but a good man." The dark pencil tip moved on to Captain Tinsley. Dad shrugged. "He's kind of high strung, a little too rough on the younger men, but I wouldn't have questioned his loyalty."

He went swiftly down the list and finally put a question mark next to two names: Sgt. Henry Krovich and Pfc. Lannie Elroy.

"I don't know, Son. I've no reason to think they aren't okay, but Krovich is a weasel, the kind of kid who always passes the buck, and Elroy is one of those blank-faced, stupid guys. You can't tell what somebody like that will do."

Dad laid down the sheet of paper. He looked at it but his gaze was abstracted. His fingers drummed a gentle rhythm on the worn oak of the table.

"I can see it all better now," he said finally. "And I see why nobody believed my story. It's the critical point of the whole thing."

"What, Mike?" Mother asked.

"It's the old magician's trick. Flap a bright scarf with one hand and nobody sees what the other hand is doing. We've all been had. Me, the CID, the Army."

"What are you talking about, Dad?"

"Misdirection," he said softly. "What was the point of the whole thing?"

"To get an M-18," I said tentatively.

"Right. And the reason everybody thinks I'm guilty is because somebody was willing to pay twenty-five thousand dollars to frame me. Now, why would anybody do that? I'm not important. I'm a good officer, but the Russians aren't interested in flushing twenty-five thousand dollars down the drain just to mess up the career of one good officer. But think what would have happened if they hadn't set up a pigeon? And set him up so good nobody could miss on the first blast."

"Well, the CID and the FBI would investigate everybody who'd been near the command post," I began slowly.

"Investigate! They'd shred through the post like locusts. And anybody who'd ever put a foot near Blue Bowl would be investigated until they knew who put braces on his teeth when he was six."

"And they'd turn up which man was a traitor!"

Dad shrugged. "They'd try hard to turn up the traitor. And the Soviets know this. So it's worth twenty-five grand to protect their man both for now and for the future."

"For the future," I repeated.

"Yes," my dad said grimly. "If they succeed in framing me, the Soviets will have an agent right in our midst. And don't bet they won't call on him again. The weapon now and maybe something as good some other day. That's worth twenty-five thousand dollars, isn't it?"

A GOOD MAN FIRST

So I had my work cut out for me. Find the weak link. Find the wobbly piece of the puzzle that the Russians were willing to pay $25,000 to protect.

I left Mother with Dad. I knew they needed some time alone together. We had our plans made and the visiting hours wouldn't run forever at the stockade. Sometimes having a kid around is like having two left feet, so I shook Dad's hand, gave Mother the car keys, and went out into the hall.

The sergeant escorted me back to the waiting room and I went out the door and down the steps in a hurry. I had a lot to do. But when I hit the sidewalk, I skidded to a stop.

I could see all the way up Pershing to the point where it joined itself again. And I could see the neat green lawns of the post hospital. All of a sudden I remembered Father Rosser. And I hadn't thought about him, not once, since Colonel Griswold had knocked on our door last night. I didn't even know if he was alive.

But I had nine men to see and one of them was a traitor.

Abruptly I turned to my left to cut across the grass to Taylor Street. I'd walk home and get my car and I'd go to Stockton Hospital and find out about Father Rosser. I could take time to see a good man before I set out to hunt a bad one.

When I reached the hospital and parked in the shade of an oak tree, I took my time getting out of the car and walking up to the broad, white steps. I don't like to visit in a hospital. The long linoleum-floored halls, the wheel chairs and crutches, the nurses in their crisp white uniforms, sick people in beds, one to a room or ten to a ward, all of it depresses me.

I didn't feel any better about it when I reached the lobby. That hospital smell—a combination of disinfectants and medicines—even reached the marbled lobby.

I walked up to the desk and a young nurse looked up and said immediately, "I'm sorry, but visiting hours are from three to five in the afternoon and seven to nine in the evening."

I looked down at my watch and it surprised me to see that it was already five-thirty. I hesitated, then asked diffidently, "Could you tell me how Father Rosser is? He was brought in last night."

Her face changed. The blank professional façade disappeared and the warmth of a person emerged.

"He's going to be all right," she said quickly. "He isn't resting too comfortably, broken ribs and a hairline crack in his right shoulder blade, but he's doing fine, really."

I smiled at her and she smiled back. Her voice was friendly and eager when she said, "You can go ahead and see him. He told Sister that no one was to be turned away. It's Room 206. Up those stairs," she pointed across the lobby, "and to the left."

The second floor was, of course, really hospital. Rooms stretched left and right. An occasional red light flashed above a door. A patient in a frayed bathrobe walked with concentrated care up the hall. Nurses moved briskly about. But it didn't get me like it usually did. Father Rosser was going to be all right.

The door to Room 206 was open. I could see him propped up on two pillows. He looked even smaller than usual. Father

Rosser was a short, spare man with wisps of white hair. I'd never seen him in anything but his clerical collar and worn black suit. Nothing about him commanded attention until you looked into his eyes. He has bright-blue eyes, eyes so clear and vivid you were sure they could see all things in heaven and on earth. There was an authority, a surety about Father Rosser that I'd never seen in another man, not even a four-star general.

He turned his head and saw me in the doorway.

"Come in, son," he called. His voice, dry and a little scratchy, always sounded like leaves skittered across cement by an autumn wind.

He held out a hand and I hurried across the little room to take it. "I'm sorry I didn't stay last night, sir. I tried to get to you, but the crowd was in the way and the policeman got there first,"

"You were right to leave. It was no place for Nancy."

His matter-of-fact reply made me feel like a man again, instead of like a deserter.

At least it did for a minute, then I blurted out the rest of it. "When I got Nancy to the car, I should have come back. I could have helped identify some of those men. But Nancy was afraid some of the MPs would recognize us, and you know what the general does if anybody on post is picked up by the police."

I stared down at the brown-and-yellow linoleum and repeated, "I should have come back."

"You would have everything be too easy, my son," he said quietly.

I looked up at him and those vivid, blue eyes were kind but measuring.

"What d' you mean?"

He started to shrug, then winced a little. "The most moral choice is not always the one which affords us the satisfaction of self-righteousness."

I frowned and tried to work out his meaning. "You think it was better for me to run away, because it would have embarrassed my dad if I'd been picked up?"

"Not just embarrass him, Bart. Give yourself more than that. And there is Kyle's death, too, and your mother's hatred of draft-dodgers and deserters. You have to balance what you want in life with its effect upon those you love. And it's never easy to know what is right."

"You don't think, then, that you should always do what you think is right, no matter what the cost?"

"Too many people are all too determined to do what they think is right without regard to God's law and to man's law." He paused and said grimly, "And they are all too ready to say their will *is* God's will."

I shook my head. "I don't understand. Last year at school everything seemed simple. It's a bad war, so we should oppose it. Father Conte helped a couple of seniors get to Canada and he led a group that messed up the Selective Service office. I thought it was great. They were willing to stand up and be counted."

I looked at the spare man propped up in the hospital bed, his night shirt rumpled, his face gray with pain, and all the time, I watched those probing bright-blue eyes.

"But it sounds to me like you think they're all wrong. So why did you lead the peace march?"

He looked at me steadily. "They have made the choice to destroy. I would like to transform. I oppose their flouting of the law to serve their ends, because the path they follow will leave freedom for no one. Not for them or for me or for those they want to help or those they want to destroy."

"But they say the only way is to tear it all down and build anew," I objected.

"Tear down, destroy," he said quietly, "that is their goal And they say that all who oppose them do so just because they benefit from the system. That isn't true. This is a sick country, my son; it must be treated, it must be cured. But when a doctor sees an inflamed hand, he doesn't kill the body, he treats the hand."

"Everything used to be so simple," I said unhappily. "When I was little, they told me this was the greatest and the best and the freest country in the world. And then I found out it wasn't true. Bombed churches in Birmingham and flame throwers and napalm bombs in little Vietnamese villages and starving children in the Appalachians. I don't know what to believe anymore."

"That is a step toward wisdom," Father Rosser said dryly.

"And at school a lot of the guys say this Red Threat business is just a myth created by the military-industrial complex to protect its own interests." I paused, "But I can't believe that. Not anymore."

And he heard the anguish in my voice. "What is it, Bart?"

"I wasn't going to bother you with it," I said miserably, "but it's my dad." And I told him all about it, all about the incredible night and day that had just passed.

His response was completely practical. "That's an excellent plan to talk with each of these men. So many times when you deal with a man you can tell if he's frightened or angry or venal. 'The tree is known by his fruits.'"

I stared at him. "So you don't have any trouble at all in believing there's a Soviet agent or maybe even a couple of them right here in Stockton."

"Of course not." He smiled a little bleakly. "I thought all you young people teethed on television. And espionage is such a familiar theme."

"Then that's another lie," I said bitterly. "All this talk about accommodation with the Soviet Union and the Russians are people, too."

"You want it to be black or white, don't you, Bart? But it isn't that simple. There's a good deal of difference between accommodation and surrender."

"If they really are our enemies, then accommodation *is* surrender."

"No," he said sharply. "Accommodation is avoiding the holocaust. The world does not belong to us, but whether we can maintain our uneasy peace with the Soviet Union may well determine the fate of the world. If we do not accommodate them and they do not accommodate us, then someday this beautiful blue ball whirling through space may be an arid, lifeless wasteland. That is what accommodation seeks to prevent."

"But what about these people who talk all the time about the Communist threat? Aren't they right—if my dad is innocent?"

"They are right if you talk about the Communist threat in terms of Soviet agents in America or Soviet aggression abroad. But they are wrong when they accuse all who disagree with them of being Communists or tools of Communists. That is the lie, Bart."

"So nobody's all right and nobody's all wrong. Is that it, Father?"

"No, Bart. There is much that is clearly wrong," he said gravely. "Communism is wrong. Those who say that after all, it is only another form of government, let them defend if they can the Berlin Wall and the Russian troops in Czechoslovakia and the killing and the pillaging by the Red Guard in China.

"And it is wrong to say that we must always give in to the Communists. The cost must be counted each time but sometimes it must be paid."

"Then why not pay it in Vietnam?"

"We have paid and paid in Vietnam," he said sadly. "And it is finally clear that victory can only come if we destroy the country utterly. So again, a choice must be made. And there are no easy answers, Bart."

He studied me. "You see, Bart, nothing is ever easy. It won't be easy for you to discover the man who framed your father. But because the way is long and difficult and you may never arrive, doesn't mean that you won't try."

"TAKE ACTION!"

On the way back to the post, I pulled into a drive-in and ordered a hamburger and Coke. I studied my list again and decided it was best to start at the top. Major Kelly lived in the BOQ. It was close to seven o'clock but maybe he stayed home on Saturday nights. I hoped so.

Dusk was settling over the post when I parked in front of the BOQ. I could see lights in the third-floor-front apartment and that was the major's.

Maybe he wouldn't want to talk to me, but Dad had said he was a good man. In a minute, I might know how right Dad was.

Major Kelly opened the door on the heels of my knock and his reddish, good-natured face broke into a smile.

"Come in, come in. You're the colonel's son, aren't you? Picture on his desk."

"Yes, sir. I'm Bart Hastings and I wondered if I could talk to you for a minute."

He reached out and grabbed my hand in a heavy hard grip. "Damn right. Glad you came. Your dad's been framed, son. You know that? I've told everybody from Colonel Griswold on, up and down, that it's a frame. Nobody'll listen to me. I was invited out to dinner tonight, but called up and said I couldn't come. Couldn't go out, with the colonel in that kind of a jam."

He stood there, short and balding and twenty pounds overweight, and I thought he was great.

"Come in and sit down, Bart. I don't know what I can do to help, but if there's anything, you name it and I'll do it. I told that captain that's going to defend Mike that I wanted to be a character witness. Some men will sell out and some won't. The colonel wouldn't."

He led the way into the living room and gestured me toward a couch which was the twin of Captain Andy's. The major pulled a straight chair away from a card table that sat in the center of the room. He turned the chair's back toward me and straddled the seat.

"I tell you," he began, "I've never been mixed up in anything like this. Nobody'll listen to me. Stayed home tonight. Thought I'd work on my stamps." He gestured at the card table and I saw the album and a pile of loose stamps and a magnifying glass. "Work on 'em when things get me down. Thought I might get an idea." He shook his head. "Haven't got any yet. I can't get anybody to open up on why they jumped on Mike. Hard to help when you don't know the facts. Once you know the facts, you assess 'em and take action. Enemy'll overrun you every time if you sit on your rear."

"Right, sir. That's what I'm trying to do. And that's where I need your help." I laid it out for him. The gun case. The bankbook, and the nine men. One of them had to be guilty.

He listened intently. His steel-gray and remarkably cold eyes never left my face. He nodded once or twice.

"Clear as a bell," he said when I'd finished. "Good concise report." And I felt like he'd just pasted a gold star on my efficiency report. I also decided the major might run off at the mouth, but he was probably a pretty tough man. Marshmallows don't have steely eyes.

"I've got the picture," he said and his voice wasn't jolly anymore. "You want to know how to find the unmarried enlisted men, the ones not listed in the post directory."

"Yes, sir."

"I'll run back to the office and get the info for you. Can I call you at home?"

"Sure. I'll be waiting there. And, Major, I want you to know that I really appreciate your help."

He pushed up from his chair. "Can it, son. I know the colonel."

I felt almost light-hearted on the way home. Major Kelly would call in a little while and I could get started seeing all the men. Then I frowned. I hadn't even thought to ask the major if he'd noticed anything odd late Tuesday or early Wednesday. I'd been too busy telling him everything I'd found out. But surely he would have told me if he'd seen anything queer.

And I wouldn't be too quick to peg him as a good guy. He was still one of the nine. I'd talk to all the men then have another look at Major Kelly.

Mother was hard at work at Dad's desk in the den when I got home. "I'm making some headway on who might have hidden the bankbook. Come look at my list," she said eagerly when she saw me in the doorway.

I walked over and looked down at the note paper. I raised my eyebrows. "Grand Central Station must have been quiet in comparison with the Hastings' quarters this week."

There were about fifteen names on the list. Three were circled.

I started to ask about them, but she said quickly, "Bart, I almost forgot! Nancy's called twice and left word for you to call her."

"Later," I said stiffly, because I remembered Nancy and her

dad dressed for tennis. Mother looked at me a little strangely, but the phone rang so I could turn away from her puzzled glance.

It was Major Kelly. "Like I thought," he began in his scrappy fashion, "Krovich, Elroy, Rodriguez, and Schwartz all live in Headquarters Company barracks, Battalion Three. That's out on Eisenhower Road."

And he gave me the addresses of Captain Tinsley and Sergeant Sanders, who lived in family housing, and of Sergeant Royce, who lived in the NCO quarters in MacArthur Square.

"Got all that?" the major asked.

"Yes, sir."

"Let me know if there's anything else I can do, son."

"I did want to ask," I said quickly, "if you saw anything odd Wednesday morning."

The pause on the phone was short, then the major said soberly, "I sure didn't, boy. Wish I had. I do know the colonel was his usual self. And I didn't see the weapon in his office." He paused again. "Saw the famous gun case, of course. Too bad I didn't look in it. Could've squashed this thing before it began."

"You didn't happen to go down to the arms room yourself?"

"No," Major Kelly said sharply. "Didn't have any business down that way. Spent the morning in the office."

I wondered if I'd offended him, but I didn't let it worry me. I might have to offend a lot of people before Dad was cleared. So I said briskly, "Well, I appreciate your help, sir." I was ready to ring off, but he spoke very quickly.

"Check back with me—after you've talked to all the men."

It was an order, not a request. And I wondered suddenly if he really was all that eager to help Dad—or if he wanted to keep tabs on me.

He misread my pause. His voice was genial when he said into

my silence, "Didn't mean to give an order there, son. But two heads are always better than one."

"Sure thing, Major. And I will check back with you."

As I hung up the phone, I smiled a little grimly. Major Kelly didn't need to worry. I wouldn't forget him—or any of the others, until Dad was cleared.

When I turned back to Mother, she was intent on her list. I looked it over again and I studied the three names she had circled. The maintenance man. The delivery man from the cleaners. The gardener.

"Why these three?"

"The others are in my garden club. It met here Tuesday afternoon. Your father said to list everyone, but I can't believe my garden club members are too likely."

I smiled. "No, not too likely. But these three. They look pretty good." I paused. I didn't want to discourage Mother but it had to be faced. "The only problem, Mom, is that you must have been in and out of the house on Tuesday and Wednesday and somebody could have got in while you were gone."

But Mother smiled serenely. "I've been busy since I got back from the stockade and I hit pay dirt when I talked to the neighbors. Mrs. Lucas, the mother of Colonel Norton next door, has been bedridden all spring with a broken hip. This last week is the first time she's been out of bed and she's spent most of the time at her window. It's at the side of the house and overlooks our quarters. And she didn't see anybody near our house except the gardener, the maintenance man, and the delivery man from the cleaners. And my bridge club, of course."

"Is she sure? I mean, what kind of old gal is she?"

"Very sensible. She's in her late sixties, very soft-spoken. She was a little embarrassed that she had seen so much of the comings and goings over here. She said, 'That's all I have time to do anymore. I can't read much and I don't like TV and it was so nice to be up and to see the street and the people coming and going.'"

"That's great, Mom. Tuesday we'll get us a private detective and have him check into these three."

It was a plus for our side. That's the way I thought of it now—our side and their side—and it seemed to me that we were gaining.

I grinned at Mother. "We'll get 'em, lady, don't you worry. Your list and my list. So now I'll go chat with some of the fellows on the list of nine."

Mother's face thinned as if the flesh had shrunk. "One of them is dangerous. Please be careful. If you learn anything, don't give it away."

She started up as if she would catch me at the door.

"Hey, Mom, get back to work on your list. Dad needs help. I can't help him by hiding in the house. And don't worry. I get the picture about our friend. Anybody who could work that kind of frame around Dad isn't to be taken lightly."

She stood, one hand outstretched.

"Don't worry, Mom," I said again. "I won't take him lightly—but I'm going to take him."

"TELL IT TO ME, BUDDY!"

Krovich and Elroy topped my list so it made sense to try the barracks first. Four of my nine lived there. On Saturday night I couldn't really hope that even one would be there, but I felt like my luck was riding tonight. Our side was gaining.

I backed the Mustang out of the driveway and went south on Grant, driving with the old two-story houses on my right and the river on my left. The headlights glanced off the reflector buttons studding the wooden railing that marked the edge of the bluff. It fell away some thirty feet to the swift-moving Kanakee River.

Grant was beginning its gradual swing to the west, leaving the river behind. I put on a spurt of speed past the officers' club and tried not to hear the faint music of the band. Saturday night and all's well. Have another drink and have you heard about Colonel Hastings.

Almost immediately I slowed down again. This was no night to be picked up by the MPs for speeding. Maybe, if I did it right, if I listened and watched men's faces as I never had before, maybe next Saturday night all would be well.

Past the club, Grant was a quiet country road. The thick tall pines crowded close to the shoulder on either side. It was another mile before the trees thinned out and lights glowed in their square windows on both sides of the road. Omaha Village, the Capehart housing for junior officers and their families, climbed up the gentle hills to my right. To my left, flowing down what once had been meadowland, was Wood Village, the family housing for NCOs. That would be where Sfc. Sanders lived. The man who found the note.

But Sergeant Sanders could wait. I wanted to see Krovich and Elroy. I stopped for a red light where Grant crossed Pershing. Ahead I could see the bright lights of the NCO club and the rows of barracks.

Battalion Three barracks filled a small valley just over the hill from the NCO club. I parked the car on the dirt shoulder across the street from Headquarters Company barracks.

It was old, World War II vintage. Wooden steps led up to a small porch. A naked bulb burned over the door, which was propped open to catch the cooling breeze that picked up in the evening in early summer.

Inside, it smelled old but recently varnished and disinfected. To the right was the CQ's room. The sergeant in charge of quarters, sprawled comfortably on a narrow bed, looked up briefly as I passed, then returned to his magazine.

Straight ahead an open door led into the barracks proper. Narrow iron cots stretched the length of the room on either side of a wide center aisle. Only a few men were there, of course. Most of them were in Stockton or at the USO or in the barracks dayroom watching TV or playing cards.

A few men lounged in the barracks itself, one writing a letter, a couple reading, one asleep, and at the far end, a guy lay quietly on top of his bed, looking at the ceiling and doing nothing. A transistor radio played softly and from the dayroom came the mumbled roar of a TV.

At the foot of each bed sat a footlocker with a soldier's name and rank stenciled on it. As I walked slowly down the aisle I spotted the names of Krovich and Elroy and Rodriguez. They weren't in. But the man at the far end of the room looking at the ceiling was Pfc. William Schwartz.

When I stood by his footlocker, I could see the book resting on his chest—*A View of the Etruscans.* He hadn't noticed my approach. I realized as I watched him that he wasn't really staring at the ceiling. He was absorbed in his thoughts.

Without any straining at all, I could see him walking casually across some campus. Long, lean, and blond, Pfc. Schwartz wasn't going to be the typical private, if there is any such thing.

"Pfc. Schwartz?" I asked.

His head lifted, then slowly he sat up.

"Yes?"

"I wonder if I could talk to you for a minute. My name is Bart Hastings. I'm Colonel Hastings' son."

His dark-brown eyes narrowed speculatively. "You want to talk to me?" He hesitated, then said abruptly, "The grapevine has it that the colonel's under arrest. Is that true?"

"Yes. But he's innocent. That's why I'm here. I thought if I talked to everybody who was out at Blue Bowl, I might pick up something the CID missed."

"Why did they arrest the colonel?" he asked quietly. "There must be a reason."

"Right. I'll level with you." And I did, because Schwartz was the kind of man who had to know the whys and wherefores.

He listened quietly, his narrow, intelligent face noncommittal and, when I'd finished, he said, "I don't mind telling what I know, which isn't much. If the colonel's guilty, it won't matter, and if he isn't, maybe this will help you."

His high forehead creased in thought. "You have to remember

that this was our first week out at Blue Bowl. We were getting it set up for the exercise to start Monday." He smiled. "Mostly, I'd been running the mimeograph machine, printing the instructions for the men of Company B on the security set up to protect the rifles."

He looked up at me. "Frankly, I can't think of anything out of the way that happened. We had a couple of Signal Corps men in Tuesday morning setting up a radio in the control room. And a maintenance man worked up in the attic awhile, but that was before the shipment arrived. And Wednesday was just another day until Sergeant Sanders came up to check about the weapon. And then, after Major Kelly called the colonel, it was really wild—CID and FBI agents and MPs everywhere."

And no matter how I went after it, that was all Schwartz could tell me. Everything was as usual. Everybody was as usual.

Then he paused and said, "The only thing a little funny on Wednesday morning was Elroy. He went into the colonel's office while the colonel was down the hall, and it seemed to me he was in there quite a while. When he came back out, I kidded him and said, 'Got a bunny stashed in there, man?' and he mumbled something about moving the colonel's bookcase. But he seemed kind of defensive."

Schwartz shrugged. "But that's no help. It was the middle of the morning and nothing happened in the colonel's office, so it's irrelevant."

"Everybody says Elroy's pretty dumb, but do you think he could have had anything to do with the theft of the rifle?"

Schwartz laughed. "Elroy a spy? Believe me, when the Russians start using people like Elroy, they'll be burying themselves, not us. No, not Elroy. No, he probably just sat down to rest for awhile in the colonel's office."

"Okay," I agreed. "Not Elroy. But how about the others?"

He looked at me soberly. "Look, Bart, I can see how it is with you. You believe in the colonel, so you think one of the rest of us has to be the man. But everybody's pretty standard. Krovich isn't likeable. He's sullen and crafty but he isn't clever. Rodriguez is just a kid. The sergeants are solid, unimaginative men, good soldiers but not much more. As for the officers, I like Major Kelly, Captain Tinsley is a pain in the neck, and Lieutenant Fagin's a big nothing, but none of them seems likely to be a traitor."

"Just as likely as my father," I said evenly.

"True enough," Schwartz said. "The whole thing seems unlikely to me—but it happened."

I felt pretty discouraged. Schwartz was smart and alert and he hadn't noticed anything odd. And if he hadn't, who would have?

"Thank you for talking to me," I said.

He shrugged. "I'm sorry I couldn't be more helpful. Do you plan to talk to everybody?"

"Yeah. I have to keep hoping that somebody saw something that'll help."

"Rodriguez and Elroy aren't in tonight, but I think I saw Krovich head for the dayroom a little while before you got here. I'll point him out to you."

I followed Schwartz through a door into a narrow hallway. It opened onto a good-sized room with a couple of card tables and some easy chairs and a TV, which was on loud enough to be heard in the next barracks.

Schwartz nodded toward a skinny guy in his middle twenties who slouched in an easy chair, his attention focused on the TV screen, then Schwartz turned and left.

I stood there for a minute and studied Krovich. His shoulders were rounded, and his hands, hooked over his knees, looked soft and flaccid. My dad had called Krovich a weasel. Schwartz said he was sullen and crafty. Krovich's face confirmed all of it.

Lank brown hair drooped over a bony forehead. A beaked nose dwarfed the small mouth and insignificant chin. Not, definitely, one of the Army's finer specimens.

I stepped around a couple of chairs and circled up to him.

"Specialist Krovich?"

He looked up indolently. "Yeah?"

"I'd like to talk to you for a minute."

He shrugged and his watery-blue eyes wandered back to the TV.

"Outside."

He looked up at me with a little more interest A frown tightened the sullen mouth, but he got up. He was used to orders. He took his time crossing the room, but he moved.

Outside on the wooden porch he leaned against the railing and pulled a pack of cigarettes from his shirt pocket. Lighting one, he blew smoke out onto the clean night air and asked, "What d' you want?"

"I want to talk to you about Blue Bowl."

The overhead light shone down harshly on Krovich's bony, acne-scarred face. His eyes flickered uneasily, like a horse facing a strange stall.

"I already told you guys everything," he said hurriedly. "What d' you want now?"

Krovich thought I was CID. So why not ride it out?

"I want to hear it again." I moved back into the deeper shadow beyond the pool of light and watched Krovich standing in the bright glare.

He hunched his shoulders forward and blustered, "I already been through it and been through it."

"Want to go in or talk here?"

Krovich licked his lips. "So okay, you want to hear it again. But I know what I'm supposed to say. You think I'm dumb?"

A warning tingled in my mind. "Tell it to me, buddy!" I said sharply.

"So okay, man," he said quickly. "Well, I got there kind of early, right on seven 'cause I got a lift out with some of the guys going on sentry. And when I got upstairs, I saw the lights were already on, but I didn't think nothin' about it. The colonel always gets there before the rest of us." He paused and giggled. "The early bird gets the worm, all right." At my lack of response, he hurried on, "So, anyway, there I am and I'm not on duty yet so I decided to go get some coffee from the pot down the hall. First one in always starts it. So I get out in the hall and I hear this noise and it sounds like somebody going down the stairs and I wondered who it was. So I hurried and looked over the bannister and I saw the colonel heading down the last flight of stairs to the basement where the arms room is."

"You saw the colonel!"

Krovich tried to back away but I was looming over him, bigger and heavier and mad. The porch railing balked him and he asked in a suddenly reedy voice, "Can't you guys make up your minds? What's with this, anyhow? First, I tell you I see this guy going down to the arms room and I can tell he's an officer. So then you want to know, couldn't it've been the colonel and I say, 'Yeah, sure, I guess it could've been,' and you guys like it real fine. Now here you are again. I don't get it."

I wanted to twist his scrawny neck. His testimony would hang my dad. It took me a minute before I could trust my hands—or my voice.

"Look, Krovich," I managed to say, "sometimes the boys get a little overanxious. I want to hear it exactly the way it was. No twists, no extras. Just give it to me straight."

He relaxed a little and started up again. "Well, it was like this. Those are old stairs, you know, and they twist around but you can see all the way to the basement. It's a real stairwell, see. So when I looked down from the second floor, this guy was already down two flights and I could just see a snatch as he made the turn to go on down to the arms room. I just got a glimpse of one side. I couldn't see his shoulder, but I could see one sleeve—and it didn't have a patch on it so it had to be an officer."

I nodded. It had to be an officer if Krovich was right. Officers wear brass on their shoulders. Enlisted men wear rank patches on their upper sleeves.

I stepped away from Krovich, back into the shadow. "So that's the way it was."

"Yeah, just like I told you guys. Then everybody kept saying, 'but didn't it look like the colonel,' and, hell, I don't know. All I saw was this guy's arm and I thought he was shorter than the colonel, but you boys kept saying the angle would make him look shorter."

He paused and frowned. "But you know something, it could've been anybody, the colonel or Major Kelly or Captain Tinsley. Even the lieutenant. I don't know who it was. But one thing—this guy moved like he was somebody."

"But that's not evidence. You remember that he looked shorter than the colonel—and you remember to tell it just the way it was at the Article 32. You understand? Just the way it was!"

KEEP THE SAVAGES AWAY

I pounded on that door like I was gouging my knuckles into Krovich's weaselly face.

"Wait a minute! I'm coming!" Captain Andy yelled.

He yanked open the door and stood framed in the doorway, big and mad, his heavy shoulders hunched, his massive hands dangling loosely at his sides.

"What the—" He recognized me and worry replaced the anger in his voice. "Bart! What's wrong? What's happened?"

"There's a lot wrong," I said angrily. "You told me you were staying right on top of the investigation, didn't you? But you didn't tell me you were setting up the defense. You didn't tell me how the Army was fixing it so Dad would be sure to hang!"

"Come on in, Bart, and spell it out for me," he said, and his voice was soft and dangerous.

I moved past him. He shut the door quietly, but there was fury in the taut line of his mouth, in the bunched muscles of his shoulders.

"I'll spell it out. I'll spell it out that the whole system stinks! You didn't tell me Friday night that Krovich had agreed to say that he saw my dad going down to the arms room early on Wednesday morning!"

Captain Andy's smoke-gray eyes narrowed, drawing his thick blond brows close together. "What do you mean, 'agreed to say' he'd seen the colonel?"

"You didn't know that I'd talk to Krovich, pin him down. That lying weasel, he told the CID he saw a man in khakis go down and it had to be an officer because he didn't have any rank on his arm, but that's all Krovich saw."

Captain Andy didn't say anything. He looked past me as if I weren't there, his face calculating, absorbed.

"That's all he saw! You couldn't hang Colonel Michael Hastings on that, so you guys jockeyed Krovich along and pretty soon, why man, he'd say it was General Loring if you smiled big when he tried it."

Captain Andy moved away from the door and walked slowly to the big easy chair. He sat down in it and shook his big head slowly back and forth. "The fools," he said tiredly. "The stupid damn fools." And the anger was gone from his face and from his big body.

I stood there in the middle of the room and I felt like an actor who'd been thrown the wrong cue. This wasn't reading right. I was going to pile it on Captain Andy and tell him that I was taking it to the general, that nobody was going to railroad my dad.

"Sit down, Bart."

I hesitated but finally walked over to the couch and sat on its edge.

He smiled faintly. "Relax, you're not really consorting with the enemy." He quirked one thick, bushy eyebrow at me and said mildly, "It made you mad when everybody believed your dad was guilty even though there was some pretty damning evidence. I'd think you wouldn't be so quick to condemn me out of hand."

I spoke and the words seemed thick in my throat. "But you didn't tell me what Krovich had said when I came here last night."

He smiled again, very faintly. "That's right. I didn't tell you because the CID didn't send over that report until this morning."

I stood up abruptly. "I'm sorry. I'm sorry," and I turned to go.

"Sit down, fella," he said again and his voice was kind, the voice of the Captain Andy that I knew—and that I should never have mistrusted.

"I'm sorry" I said again. "I should have known—"

He waved me to silence. "That's okay. I can see why you got confused. I told you I was staying on top of the investigation. And I am. But that means I'm having the CID send me a copy of all the sworn statements. JAG officers don't investigate. That's CID's job."

"But these statements, they go to the investigating officer. So he'll think Krovich saw Dad! Then Krovich'll testify—"

Captain Andy shook his head. "No, he won't! I'll have a little talk with Krovich and point out to him what the penalty for perjury is and he'll decide to make a fresh sworn statement. I'll fix it."

"But what if he gets up on the witness stand and tells his made-up story anyway?"

"Captain Brody can call you as a witness and impeach his testimony. So don't worry about it, Bart."

I did sit down then, because my legs felt like a couple of pieces of cooked macaroni.

"I was scared! When I found out what he was going to say, I was terrified! That kind of testimony could hang Dad! What if I hadn't talked to Krovich?"

Then I got mad all over again. "What good is the law when that can happen to a man? What kind of a lousy system do we live under?"

He looked at me, his eyes bright and angry, "It's odd, isn't it, how the shoe can pinch when it's your own foot."

"What are you talking about?"

"Law and order's a dirty word, isn't it—until somebody breaks a law and it's your rights that get trampled. Those CID sergeants were breaking the law when they led Krovich like that. And it makes you pretty mad, doesn't it? But how about the lawbreakers on the campus? That's something else again, isn't it?"

"Sure it is," I said hotly. "They want freedom!"

"For themselves maybe, but not for anybody else."

"That's not true!"

"Isn't it?" he asked shortly. "They march and they riot and break up furniture and people and burn down libraries and that's okay. In fact, it's their God-given right because they are doing it for something they believe in. But let me tell you something, buddy, the man who led the mob against the peace march in Stockton Friday night believed in what he was doing, too. So if it's okay for you people to march and fight and destroy and ignore the law, then it's okay for the mob leader—and for the overeager CID sergeants. Isn't it?"

He pushed up out of his chair and paced the floor. "And that way lies savagery. Don't you see, Bart? The law is the only thing that holds civilization together. And without it, the world is a jungle, and twice as dangerous, because the predator is man."

"But sometimes the law is wrong!"

"Then work to change it," he shot back. "What happens when two-hundred-twenty million people choose which laws they are going to obey?"

"Sometimes you have to be true to your conscience."

He smiled grimly. "What about other people's consciences? Like it or not, you're a member of a community. If you really wish it well, want it to work, then you work with other members of the community to cure the evils. But that's a good deal harder to do than to ignore or break the law."

He ran a massive hand through his thick blond hair and sighed tiredly. "I don't know how to make it any clearer, Bart. But if we lose the law, we've lost civilization. And the law is a fragile thing. It's there to protect everybody and without it—"

"—there's no freedom for anybody," I said slowly.

"That's right. You think about it, Bart. Is it to be freedom for everybody—or just for the people who agree with you?"

"Captain Andy, on the campus they believe in what they are fighting for and they think the only way to make government respond is to use force. They've seen the law used against people too many times."

He nodded. "I know what you mean. It's like the CID sergeants leading Krovich along. That's perversion of the law." His eyes sad and thoughtful, he said, "The law is undermined from all sides. Men who subvert it and men who don't wish to see it truly enforced. There are so many who don't want the law to be what it was meant to be. You know how the hate groups attacked Chief Justice Warren for so many years? They did it because he insisted the law was meant for everybody, rich and poor, black and white."

I laughed a little. "I'd always heard the law was a jealous mistress—but I didn't know she was an all-consuming passion."

He grinned. "I keep a soapbox hidden in the bedroom. But I mean what I say. The law is going to do its part to protect your father, too. You can count on that. All you have to do is keep up the good work. You see the rest of the men, Bart. Dredge up whatever you can and take it to Captain Brody. He's defense counsel."

"I'll do it. You can count on that," I said grimly. I pushed up from the couch. "And I'll start now. Lieutenant Fagin lives right downstairs."

"REMEMBER KROVICH!"

Lieutenant Fagin blocked the door to his quarters. He stood there, tall, lean, and natty in his checkered Bermudas and pale-blue polo shirt, and just about as responsive as a block of granite.

I said it again. "I'm Colonel Hastings' son and I want to talk to all the men who were out at Blue Bowl on Tuesday and Wednesday. You see, there might be something that somebody—" His abrupt headshake stopped me cold.

"Why not?"

"I've been instructed not to discuss the case."

"Instructed by whom?"

"The CID."

"What can it hurt if you talk to me?"

"I've had my instructions. I intend to obey them."

And the door shut in my face.

I stood there in the hall. Lieutenant Fagin was Regular Army, a West Point man. I thought of Captain Andy's dad, who knew when to follow orders, and I thought *I'd rather have a field commander like General Brainard than a robot-like Lieutenant Fagin.* But I didn't get mad. He was trying to do what he thought was right.

I clattered down the steps of the BOQ. It was almost ten and I knew I'd been at it too long. Even if I could track down another of the nine, I had played out for the night. I drove out Grant, but almost automatically the car started to slow when I reached General Loring's quarters.

Light spread softly through the draped windows of the living room and shone cheerfully from the kitchen in the back. I had pulled into the circular drive and parked without making any conscious decision, but as the motor fell silent, I knew I needed to see Nancy.

She met me at the front door.

"I hoped you would come tonight, Bart." Her vibrant dark eyes softened. "You look tired. Come on out to the kitchen. I've been making cookies."

Once in the kitchen, with light spilling on the shining floor and the aroma of fresh cookies and Nancy, Nancy of the soft-silk hair and the lovely long legs in brief yellow shorts, it suddenly seemed like a beautiful night and I wasn't tired any longer.

I drank three glasses of milk and ate a plateful of cookies and told her everything, from our talk with Dad to my visit with Father Rosser to the questioning of Schwartz and Krovich and my confrontation with Captain Andy.

That took some of the edge off the night.

"Yeah, I made a fool out of myself. I all but accused Captain Andy of fixing the case and he read me up one side and down the other. And then I went downstairs and met up with Mr. Duty himself."

"Don't tell me," she said quickly. "I'll bet I know. The estimable Lieutenant Fagin. Right?"

"How did you know?"

"Lieutenant Fagin plays tennis with my father every Saturday. Dad says he doesn't suffer bores gladly but Fagin is the best tennis player on the post—except for Dad, of course. You know how Dad is about tennis."

"So that's why you went to the club," I said before I thought.

"You knew?"

"Mother and I saw you when we were on the way to the stockade."

She reached across the table and took my hand. "Oh Bart, you thought I was just going out to play. Didn't you?"

I held tight to her hand. "This is my night to learn. Captain Andy and you. I'm sorry, Nancy."

"But you came tonight?"

"I couldn't stay away," I said simply.

"Don't ever stay away, Bart." And then, quickly, she pulled free her hand and reached for the milk carton to pour me another glass.

"Don't," I objected. "I'll moo if I drink anymore. Tell me how you vamped Lieutenant Fagin." Then I said seriously, "Did you find out anything? He wouldn't give me the time of day."

She frowned. "I'm not sure." An impish smile flitted over her face and her dark eyes gleamed. "I knew he was on your list and having heard Dad talk I didn't think Quentin would be too cooperative." She grinned. "I'll bet he has to have an order signed in triplicate before he takes a coffee break. Anyway, when he and Dad finished playing, I was right there, admiring Quentin's skill and his backhand and all the bit."

She grinned again, "Dad was mystified. He knows I don't date anyone but you, but he's a gallant old dear and I suppose he thought if I wanted to play the field I couldn't have picked, from his viewpoint, a safer playmate. So with a good deal of heavy-handed tact he left Quentin and me alone with Cokes at a pool-side table and slipped away.

"I worked it around to the disappearance of the M-18 and said Dad had been particularly impressed with the report that Quentin had made to the CID. I said Dad had praised it as a model of concise and clear-headed thoroughness. And, eventually of course, with a good deal of encouragement, Quentin was persuaded to give me a verbatim account of exactly what he had told the CID."

"And what did he tell them?"

"He arrived a little before seven on Wednesday morning. He didn't leave his office until it was time for lunch, then he drove to the officers' mess. He spoke to your father twice that morning. He said the colonel's manner was as usual."

My shoulders slumped. "That doesn't help much."

"I know. I kept after him. I asked if there had been anything at all out of the ordinary. Anything. He frowned and I pounced on it. I kept stressing what a fine sense of observation he had and what a good witness he had been, and he finally came out with one odd thing."

"What?"

"He heard a noise up above him right around seven o'clock."

"Up above—but that's the attic!"

"I know, and I don't see how it could tie in. He said he heard this scraping noise and a kind of light thump and that was all. He listened for a minute but nothing more happened, so he forgot about it. He said it was probably pack rats."

I frowned and said, "Yeah, probably so. But I'm glad you talked to him. It adds to the picture." Then I sighed and shook my head. "Nancy, I don't think I'm getting anywhere."

"What do you mean?"

"This afternoon I thought it was a great idea to talk to all the men. Father Rosser thought so, too. He said, 'The tree is known by his fruits.' But I guess I'm just not smart enough to see it. I talk to these guys and I can't picture any of them as the all-powerful superspy we keep talking about. I think I'm just running around in circles."

"Oh no," she said quickly. "Remember Krovich!"

"Krovich?"

"Bart, if you hadn't talked to him his testimony would've hung your dad! And who knows what else you will find out when you talk to the rest of the men."

And she was right. Maybe I wouldn't be able to point a finger and yell, 'That's the man!' when I'd talked to all of them, but who knew what else I might learn.

"Yeah," I said grimly, "I won't forget Krovich. You're right, Nancy. I'll keep after it."

But I was scared, scared it would all come to nothing, and Nancy knew I was scared. She reached across the table and took my hand. I held hers tightly.

"Nan, if you'd seen Dad this afternoon! I've never seen him beaten, not even when Kyle died. That was bad but he had something to hold onto. Kyle was an officer and he was doing his duty. But today, Dad didn't have anything 'til Mother and I gave him some hope that somehow, someway, we'd figure it out."

I held onto Nancy's hand like it was a lifeline. "I've just got to come up with something!"

A LIFE GRENADE

"Laxity," the captain said venomously. "Just another case of laxity! Too much mollycoddling these days. Soldiers aren't what they used to be. And these young officers. . . ." Captain Tinsley was too indignant to speak—or perhaps he had lost the thread of his argument. His light eyes glittered and his bony forefinger ground into my chest. He pulled himself together and leaned back a little on the sofa, and I felt a pang of sympathy for Lieutenant Fagin. No wonder he toed the line.

Captain Tinsley was only too eager to talk about the rifle theft. But, out of his spew of words, I hadn't picked up one useful fact and now I was wondering how I was going to get out of there.

I looked around the living room of his quarters. Everything was in place. Not one loose page from the Sunday comics littered the floor. The ashtrays sat precisely two inches from the edge of each end table. The lamps matched down to the last twirling flower on the shades. I began to feel like I was suffocating.

"Sir, I really appreciate your talking to me on a Sunday morning," I said, and I started to stand up. That bony forefinger pinned me again.

"Listen, boy, you mark my words," and he leaned so close I could see the fillings in his yellowed teeth. "You mark my words, it was an inside job. Somebody framed the colonel. Clear as the nose on your face." He moved even a little closer. "And don't say I said so, but I'd take a pretty close look at that Irishman."

"Irishman?" I said blankly, leaning as far back into the cushions as I could.

His eyes darted first one way and then the other, then he whispered conspiratorially, "Kelly." Then he bounced to his feet and I got up quickly, too. Brother, did I want out of there, and fast.

The captain padded along with me as I edged toward the door, and now his eyes were anxious. "Of course, that's only between the two of us. Just a little hint."

I stopped at the front door and asked abruptly, "Why him?"

"He's too jolly, just too damned jolly," and again the captain's voice was edged with venom. I looked at him, standing in the bright shaft of summer sun in the open doorway, and I knew why he hated 'that Irishman'. Tinsley was old to be a captain, too old. When had he been passed over? And how soon would he face mandatory retirement? Not a minute too soon for the sake of the Army.

But I didn't brush him off. Instead, I thanked him again and shook his hand and smiled. When I got to the car I felt like I'd walked out of dark dankness onto a clean wind-swept hilltop.

When I found Pfc. Rodriguez busily shining his shoes in Headquarters Company barracks of Battalion Three, his bright, welcoming grin reassured me that lots and lots of people are perfectly normal.

Rodriguez's big spaniel-brown eyes grew serious when I introduced myself and his mobile mouth dropped with sympathy.

"Jeez, mister, I wish I could help. I like your old man. He's nice to everybody." Rodriguez ruffled his curly black hair and squinted his eyes in thought. "Jeez, what makes it tough, it was like any morning. The old man, he works in his office, makes a lotta phone calls. He had me pinnin' up a big map. Then I was workin' down the hall, settin' up a room for files."

Rodriguez brightened. "I can tell you this, the colonel didn't go down the stairs all morning."

I gripped his shoulder. "Are you sure?"

"Not from the time I got there," he said eagerly.

"When was that?"

"At 0800. That's when I go on duty."

My hand slipped off his shoulder. "That doesn't help. The critical time is from 0700 to 0800."

"Jeez, mister, I'm sorry."

And he really was. His black brows drew together and he slumped dolefully.

I grinned down at him. "Anyway, thanks a lot. And if you think of anything, let me know. Okay?"

He promised to call if anything occurred to him, and when I left him hard at work again on his shoes, I was grateful. He hadn't helped me in my quest, but he had sure reaffirmed my faith in the human race.

Elroy tipped the scales back toward negative when I talked to him. He was slouched in the dayroom, dully watching a baseball game on TV.

It wasn't that Elroy was nuts like Captain Tinsley, but he couldn't think his way to a complete sentence. We went out on the porch where I'd talked to Krovich the night before, and in comparison Krovich had been a golden-tongued orator.

"Wednesday morning?" he repeated slowly. "Nothin' happened Wednesday morning."

I couldn't believe it! I said gently, "You know that an M-18 is missing?"

He frowned. "The colonel took one of the weapons and didn't put it back, so he's in trouble. That's what Sergeant Sanders said."

I almost dropped it there. Elroy didn't even understand what Dad was accused of doing. I could understand why the captain had Elroy moving and lifting things. Elroy would probably disintegrate if anybody asked him to file papers.

But I asked him to tell me what he had done on Wednesday morning. I took him over it slowly and when he'd finished I had only what I had known when I started. He'd come on duty, he'd moved files, he'd rearranged some furniture, and he hadn't been downstairs.

"Everybody said the colonel was in his office all morning. Is that right?"

"No. He went down the hall to the coffee machine once."

And I wondered why Elroy remembered that.

"Was he gone long?" I asked cautiously.

"A while."

"What were you doing in his office while he was gone?"

For the first time, something flickered in his eyes. Then he said hastily, "Nothin'."

"You must have been doing something," I said easily.

He stared at me. "Movin' the bookcase."

And that was all I got. The only other burst of animation came when I asked Elroy if he'd ever seen an M-18.

"Yeah," he said softly. "She's beautiful, real beautiful. Holds in your hand like a baby, sweet and light. Man, I wanted to shoot her." Then his heavy face darkened. "They laughed and said I couldn't 'cause it was only the special company that was going to shoot her. But, man, I'm a Sharpshooter. I can shoot better than anybody. I don't know why they ever made me an office soldier."

And when I looked at him, big and powerful and muscular, I wondered where the computer had slipped up. Out in the boondocks, Elroy would be a good man. But he sure wasn't meant to be a clerk.

"Well," I said lamely, "maybe you can get a transfer."

His big face smoothed out. "The colonel said he'd work on it." He frowned. "I sure hope they don't stay mad at the colonel. He said he was going to help me. I hope he gets back to the office real soon."

"I hope so, too," I said steadily.

I left Elroy standing on the small wooden porch staring blankly after me. When I reached the Mustang and climbed in, I hesitated, undecided what to do next. It was almost three o'clock and I had an appointment at five at the stockade with Captain Brody and Dad. I only had the two sergeants left to see but I wasn't sure I could manage both in the time left.

Sanders or Royce, which would it be? Royce lived nearest in the NCOQ for bachelor noncoms, but Sanders was the sergeant in charge of the arms room. I opted for Sanders.

The NCO married housing spread down a meadow below the hillside Capeharts for officers' families. And it wasn't quite as nice. Not anything too obvious. The houses were modern, neat duplexes, but the sidings were frame, not brick, and the design completely utilitarian.

I drove slowly as I swung into the area. Kids swarmed everywhere, flying kites, kicking balls, and just plain running. I took a quick look at the addresses on my list, turned right up a dead end, and stopped at the last duplex.

Sfc. Timothy Sanders' name was neatly stenciled on the left-hand duplex. In its parking slot, I could see the feet of a man sticking out from beneath a '66 Ford coupe, and hear a muffled whistling.

As I got out of my car, he pulled himself from beneath the coupé, sat up at a toolbox, and began to rummage, still whistling cheerfully to himself.

I walked up to him and asked, "Sergeant Sanders?"

He looked up, squinting against the sunlight. His broad face was smeared with grime, but good-humored.

"That's my name," he said equably.

"I'm Bart Hastings, Colonel Hastings' son." I got that far and stopped. His face hardened and he no longer looked happy.

"Yeah," he said flatly.

I stumbled through my piece. He looked at me stolidly all the while, then in one abrupt motion, he stood.

"Look, kid, I don't have anything to say but what I'm sayin' tomorrow at the 32. I find a note, see, and it's from the colonel so I do what it says. I follow my orders. And there's not anybody gonna tell me the colonel didn't write that note 'cause I know his handwritin', see?"

I saw, all right. The sergeant felt like he was in a corner. He was defensive and angry, because somebody had got away with one of his weapons. And nobody was going to convince him that note was a forgery.

When I left, he stared after me, too, not blankly, but with the angry fighting look of a man who's scared somebody is going to blame him.

I almost said to heck with it. I thought about Nancy and a cool quick swim at the officers' club. There'd be time before I needed to meet with Captain Brody and Dad. But when the car reached Grant, I turned left instead of right and headed back toward the battalion barracks.

As I waited on the light at Pershing, I thought I was being kind of stupid. Sanders had been a wash-out. What did I expect to get from the other sergeant? But I had set out to see all nine men and I was going to do it.

The NCO quarters was a square frame building at the top of a rise. The small plain foyer was cool and shadowy. I checked the roster for Sergeant Ed Royce's room. When I reached the second floor and knocked at Number 26, I thought I was out of luck. But I waited a minute and knocked again.

I was turning away when a stubble-faced guy about forty poked his head out of the next room.

"Lookin' for Ed Royce?"

I nodded.

"He's out back. With the flowers."

I kind of looked at him for a minute, then said a quick thank you and started back downstairs. I wondered if I could possibly have heard right, but when I rounded the corner of the building I got the picture.

Shirtless, wearing old khaki pants, Sergeant Royce knelt by a flower bed. He was tanned a golden bronze, and the muscles in his broad back rippled as he leaned across a bed of petunias to gouge out an offending dandelion.

The sloping grounds behind the building would have brought gasps of envy from little-old-lady gardeners anywhere. A semicircular bed of flowers curved around of the lawn. Pansies and petunias, daffodils and tulips flowered purple and pink, yellow and red. In the sleepy quiet of a Sunday afternoon, it was an enchanted picture—the rippling muscles in a powerful back and the vibrant colors of the flowers, nature's best on display.

The thick green grass was springy underfoot. More of the sergeant's work, I was willing to bet. The Army doesn't run to golf-course grass behind NCO quarters.

I had moved only a couple of feet across the grass when the sergeant's head jerked around. He couldn't have heard my soft footfalls. He had sensed movement behind him. This was the sort of sergeant you'd like to have along in a rice paddy.

When I explained who I was, he stood and shook my hand.

He was as tall as Captain Andy and even more impressive. He moved with the ease of a superbly-conditioned athlete.

"Are you trying to find out who stole the M-18?" he asked abruptly.

It took me completely by surprise. "Then you don't think my dad—"

"Somebody hoked it up," he said briefly. "The whole thing smells. I've been in the Army for seventeen years and I've served under a lot of men, most of them pretty good. Your dad's one of the best. Come on and sit down. Let me see if I can help."

We sat on the grass. The smell of the freshly-upturned earth in the flower bed mingled with the thick scent of honeysuckle. The bright warmth of the sun baked down on us.

I went through my piece about talking to all of the men, hoping for some scrap of information that might help Dad.

He grinned, and his lean hawk-nosed face looked a little less predatory. "I'd talk to us, too," he said dryly, "because one of us stole that weapon."

"How do you figure?" I asked, scarcely daring to breathe.

"Nobody but us chickens was in the roost and I've talked to the K-9 boys who patrolled that Tuesday night. They said their dogs would have spotted a field mouse, so that puts it back in headquarters."

"Do you know something, Sergeant? I've talked to everybody but you're the only one who's pinned it down to the nine of you. What else have you figured out?"

He looked at me from under his thick black brows and said, "One thing. If the colonel didn't take the M-18 out in his gun case and nobody else took out a package big enough to hold a weapon, then where do you suppose the rifle is?"

I had waited tensely as he started speaking but his question disappointed me. He wasn't so smart, after all. "That's what everybody's been trying to figure out," I said shortly.

"If nobody took the rifle out, where is it?" he repeated softly.

And then I understood and I felt like he'd tossed me a live grenade.

TO TELL OR NOT TO TELL

I drove around aimlessly for a while after I left Sergeant Royce. We'd made a plan, but the whole thing scared me. If the thief got the gun out. . . . But we'd gone over it and over it. There wasn't any other way if we were going to save Dad.

The car seemed to head toward the BOQ by itself. I pulled into an empty parking place mid-way up the block and stared at the gray wooden buildings.

I could go up to Captain Andy's quarters. I could tell him how Sergeant Royce and I had it figured, that the weapon had never left Blue Bowl, that it had to be hidden somewhere in the compound. But Captain Andy would immediately alert Colonel Antonelli, the judge advocate, and the colonel would call the general.

No, by God. Sergeant Royce and I had decided what to do. I'd run it out.

No, I wouldn't go see Captain Andy, but since I still had forty-five minutes before I was due at the stockade to talk with Dad and Captain Brody, I'd see if Major Kelly was in his quarters. He had asked me, ordered me, to check back with him. So I would. If he wanted to keep tabs on me, I'd oblige him. I might learn something from him. And maybe—if I felt he really wanted to help Dad—maybe I could ask him what he thought about the plan Sergeant Royce and I had made.

The major was in. "Got any news, boy?" he asked immediately.

"Not much. I've talked to everybody. I thought maybe, if you weren't busy, we could go over it together."

"Sure, sure." He motioned me to the divan, and while I laid it all out, he paced up and down in front of the empty fireplace, his head bent in thought. He listened hard. He didn't miss anything.

And, of course, he pounced on the bit about Krovich.

"So he backed down when you jumped on him? Said it wasn't your father, after all?"

"When I pushed him hard enough, he folded right up. All he really saw was a sleeve. He was just trying to please the CID by saying it was Dad."

The major paused in his pacing and looked down at me. "Son, you did your father a great service when you wrung the truth out of Krovich! Why, that testimony would have put your father in Leavenworth!"

"It could have finished him," I said grimly. I took a deep breath. "So I learned quite a bit, really. Krovich is a liar. Elroy's stupid. Captain Tinsley is a nut. Lieutenant Fagin is a jerk. Pfc. Schwartz is smart. Sergeant Royce can think." I paused and smiled. "And I like Rodriguez." Then the smile faded. "But I haven't proved anything. And I still don't know who stole the rifle."

"I'd say you're a lot further along than that!" the major rejoined.

I felt a quick flash of hope. Had he seen something that I'd overlooked?

"How?"

The major nodded his round face emphatically. "I'd say that you've come up with a real suspect. Krovich!"I felt abruptly let down. "Krovich is just a weasel. He saw somebody. . . ." my voice trailed off at Major Kelly's impatient headshake.

"Think, son! Didn't it ever occur to you that the man going down the stairs might have been Krovich himself! The story could have been to cover himself in case anybody got a glimpse of him near the stairs. And that's why he said the sleeve didn't have a rank patch! I think you ought to investigate him real hard."

I nodded slowly. The major might have something. After the Article 32, when we hired the private detective to check on all the men, I could have him take a close look at Krovich.

"Krovich is a real possibility," I agreed. Then I shrugged. "But so is everybody. Major, is there anything else you can think of that might help? Anything odd or out of the ordinary about any of the men?"

Major Kelly's round face creased in thought. His thick, sandy eyebrows bunched over his cold gray eyes. A long moment passed.

I studied him—the cold gray eyes and the reddish good-natured face. He was bouncy and he talked like an old Army movie, but, I thought, his staccato manner reflected a very quick and alert mind.

Could it have been the mind that planned the theft and the trap for Dad?

I didn't know.

The thief could just as easily be Captain Tinsley, paying back the system that had passed him over. Or it could be the enigmatic Lieutenant Fagin, playing the role of a stuffy, unimaginative robot.

It might even be the charming and likeable Rodriguez, masking cold calculation with ingenuous smiles. Or it could be Krovich, not a weasel but a fox. Or maybe Sergeant Sanders, scared because he might be blamed.

I didn't think, though, that it could be Elroy. Nobody can pretend to be that stupid. And I trusted Sergeant Royce. I knew that Dad hadn't taken the M-18 out in his gun case. And if it didn't go out in Dad's gun case, the M-18 was still in Blue Bowl HQ. And Royce couldn't be the thief, because the thief would never even hint at the true hiding place of the weapon.

So I had the possibilities figured. But I still waited hopefully for Major Kelly to speak. After all, he was the exec. He should know the men better than anybody.

Finally, though, he looked at me soberly and said, "I'm sorry, boy. I can't think of anything peculiar. If I were you, I'd just concentrate on Krovich."

"Right, sir," I said quickly and I hid my disappointment. I shouldn't have expected any miracles, anyway.

I hesitated. Should I tell him about the weapon still being in Blue Bowl?

The major misunderstood the indecision in my face and repeated bullishly, "Krovich. That's the ticket, son."

And I decided that I couldn't jeopardize the plan that Sergeant Royce and I had devised by telling it to the major. Major Kelly had promised to help in any way he could. But he was awfully quick to try and put the finger on Krovich. Was it because he truly thought Krovich the guilty one? Or was it because Krovich said he saw an officer going down the steps to the arms room and that brought it too close to the major for comfort?

I didn't know. I only knew that I couldn't share the burden of the M-18's hiding place. I couldn't trust anybody.

The decision to keep quiet about the rifle still being in Blue Bowl was mine to make—and mine to carry all by myself.

THE ARTICLE 32 BEGINS

So I kept quiet about the weapon all of Sunday afternoon and Sunday night, and I still carried the secret on Monday morning as Mother and I climbed the worn wooden stairs to the second floor of the JAG building.

As we walked toward the courtroom, the narrow hallway seemed full of men. Two long wooden benches sat near the doors to the courtroom and both benches were full. I recognized almost everyone—the nine men who had been in Blue Bowl that morning, the CID men who had come to our quarters—but a few of the faces were strange.

Major Kelly sat at the end of one bench. As we passed, I said, "Good morning, sir," but I barely had the words out when an MP snapped, "No talking to the witnesses, please."

So I nodded and walked on. My eyes paused on the rugged face of Sergeant Royce. He saw me and nodded infinitesimally. My hands were suddenly sweaty. The sergeant's nod meant that he had passed on, as if from higher authority, an order to the sentries at Blue Bowl that every vehicle and every package that left the command post was to be searched. But even so, the sergeant and I were taking a terrific risk if our guess was right and the M-18 was still somewhere in the command post.

At the closed doors to the courtroom, two MPs stood guard, admitting only those possessing special chits prepared by the JAG office. So it was still under wraps that a full colonel was thought to be the villain. Of course, it wasn't a real secret on post but so far it hadn't leaked to the newspapers off post. The public pillory would begin if the Article 32 investigation recommended a court-martial. Then it would be headline news from coast to coast.

A short stubby MP took our chits, checked them carefully against a typewritten flimsy, then nodded to the second MP, who swung open the doors and let us pass.

I'm no authority on courtrooms, but you knew where you were the minute you passed through the doors of this one.

Four rows of yellow wooden benches sat on either side of a narrow center aisle. Beyond the first row a plain wooden railing marked off the area for the court. On a dais at the front of the room sat a long wooden structure like an oversized judge's bench. It had to be long to accommodate the nine chairs behind it. Nine men sit on a court-martial. Today the bench gleamed in the soft light from the windows, its surface shining and empty except for a single pad of white paper in front of the middle chair.

Mother faltered as we started down the aisle, her eyes fixed wide on that raised bench with the flag of the United States on one side and the flag of Fort Calhoun on the other. In only a few minutes, Colonel Anton Krueger would take his place behind that bench to inquire into the truth of the charge against Colonel Michael Hastings.

I took her elbow and we walked on down the aisle to the first row. We sat on the left side of the aisle. Just past the railing, only a few feet in measure but so far away, was the table for the defense. A tan briefcase sat by one of the two wooden chairs. Two legal pads rested on the table.

Mother stared straight ahead, her face pale and set. Her hands gripped her purse so tightly that her knuckles had whitened. It was very quiet in the courtroom. I looked around and realized that there would be no spectators in the usual sense. I saw a couple of civilians and I wondered if they were FBI agents. But all the principals in the case were out in the hall and I guessed they would stay there until called to testify.

But I was thankful for the empty courtroom. The fewer there, the less likelihood there was of the story being leaked to the press. And I could still hope that a miracle would happen and the Article 32 would clear Dad.

I wondered all over again if I'd been wrong to sit on the theory that Sergeant Royce and I had worked out. The night before, I'd been tempted to tell Captain Brody and Dad. But I knew my father. He would insist upon alerting the CID and they would tear the command post apart hunting for the M-18. And if they found it, it wouldn't help Dad because of the $25,000. We had to get the man who had hidden the rifle.

So I juggled the grenade. Somehow I had to set a trap that would bring the shadowy thief out from his cover. But how?

Then a door opened behind the dais. Captain Brody, slight and boyish, led the way. Behind him, tall and grave, came my father. They crossed in front of the dais and walked to the defense table.

I was proud of Dad. He was every inch an infantry officer from the airborne ranger insignia to the thick rows of service ribbons on his chest. He moved confidently, easily. When he reached the table, he stopped and smiled at Mother, his dark eyes warm. And when he sat down, his shoulders and the back of his neck radiated confidence.

Dad was okay.

I looked down at my watch. Ten minutes to go.

Just then Captain Andy came through the same door, a sheaf of papers in his hand. I watched him take his place at the table on the right and my emotions tangled up.

Captain Andy, big, blond, and impressive, was the enemy now. He was there to assist Colonel Krueger, to help the government, not Dad.

At precisely 0900 hours, Colonel Anton Krueger walked into the courtroom and quietly took his place in the center chair behind the court-martial bench on the dais.

A good many men might look ridiculous behind a long empty desk backed by eight empty chairs, but not Colonel Krueger. A medium-sized man with thinning sandy hair, he meticulously arranged a thick stack of papers then looked up and quietly surveyed the courtroom—and everyone in it immediately felt the impact of his personality. Thin-lipped, unsmiling, hollow-cheeked, his face was severe, his bearing assured.

He began without preamble, his clear, colorless voice even and unemotional.

"Pursuant to instructions issued by the commanding general and in accordance with Article Thirty-two of the Uniform Code of Military Justice, I am opening the investigation into the theft of a classified weapon from Third Battalion temporary command post in Blue Bowl sector on Wednesday four June nineteen sixty-nine.

"Under military law, the theft of classified material and its transfer to a foreign power constitutes treason. The purpose of this investigation is to provide a recommendation to the commanding general as to whether there is sufficient evidence to warrant court-martial proceedings against the accused, Colonel Michael Alan Hastings."

He paused and looked down at my father.

"Will the accused please stand?"

My father rose and stood at attention.

"It is my duty to inform you of the charge against you," Colonel Krueger began. "You are accused of stealing and purveying to hostile foreign agents an M-18 rifle. The charge is treason. It is also my duty to inform you that you or your counsel have the right to present evidence in your behalf and to examine all witnesses testifying in this investigation. It is also your right, Colonel Hastings, to remain silent. If you should choose to testify, the government will have the right to cross-examine. Does the accused have any questions?"

"No, sir," my father replied clearly.

"Very well then. I will call the first witness—" He broke off as Captain Andy rose and approached the dais. Captain Andy spoke quietly then returned to his seat.

Colonel Krueger looked over at the defense table. "Does the defense have any objection to the closing of the courtroom to the public?"

Captain Brody rose. "No, sir. No objection."

Colonel Krueger looked back down at his papers and made a brief note.

So Captain Andy was the watchdog, making sure that everything went according to Hoyle.

Colonel Krueger again addressed the defense. "After each witness has testified, he will be seated in the courtroom in case I wish to recall anyone. Does the defense object?"

Captain Brody thought for a minute, then shook his head. "No objection, sir."

"At this time I will call Colonel William Griswold to the stand."

A private from the JAG office got up at the rear of the courtroom and called the colonel in from the hall and the Article 32 was under way.

THE EVIDENCE PILES UP

Colonel Griswold, his thickly-fleshed face somber, moved heavily down the aisle. At the front of the courtroom, he stopped in front of the dais, faced the bench, and held up his right hand. Colonel Griswold knew the drill, obviously.

Colonel Krueger, his right hand also up, intoned, “Do you swear to tell the truth, the whole truth, and nothing but the truth, so help you God?”

“I do.”

“Please take the witness stand and state your name, rank, and serial number.”

And so the formal machinery of the Article 32 began to move. At a desk to the left and below the dais sat the court reporter, a slight, gray-haired sergeant. He was transcribing every word that was said. The record was being made.

“I have here the report of the CID’s investigation, colonel. Would you please describe to me the steps taken by the CID.”

Colonel Griswold laid it out, the arrival of the M-18s, the safe accounting of all of them, the note found on Wednesday morning, the sergeant’s query when the gun wasn’t returned, the gun case, the CID’s search of our quarters, the discovery of the bankbook, and the decision to take Dad into custody.

Colonel Krueger zeroed in on the bankbook. "What have you since discovered about this bankbook, Colonel?"

"According to the information forwarded to us by the FBI, the account was opened by letter on May twenty-first with a check of twenty-five thousand dollars. The letter was signed and the check was endorsed by Mitchell Harmon. The initials are the same as those of the accused, Michael Hastings, and the handwriting appears to be that of the accused with some attempt at disguise."

"Has the source of the twenty-five thousand dollars been identified?"

"Yes, sir. The money paid into the account of one Mitchell Harmon came from an organization known as The United World, Incorporated. It is on the Attorney General's list of subversive organizations."

Colonel Krueger paused and wrote on his note pad. Then his cold, blue eyes turned on Captain Brody.

"Does the defense wish to cross-examine?"

"Yes, sir." Captain Brody rose and walked slowly toward the witness stand, his head bent as if in thought. Then he looked up at Colonel Griswold and said sharply, "Colonel, you have testified that the letter opening the savings account appears to be the handwriting of the accused. Who says that 'it appears to be' Colonel Hastings' handwriting?"

"FBI agent John Cravens, a forgery expert."

"Is that all that Agent Cravens reported?"

"No, Captain, that is not the extent of his report."

"What precisely did Agent Cravens say about that signature?"

"He said that it could have been written by Colonel Hastings with some attempt at disguise or that it could be a forgery intended to give that impression."

"In other words, Colonel, the signature could be a forgery

deliberately intended to look like Colonel Hastings' handwriting semi-disguised? Is that correct?"

"Yes."

"So we don't know who signed that letter, do we, Colonel?"

"No, Captain."

"The money itself," Captain Brody said quietly. "You've traced it to a subversive organization, is that right?"

"Yes, sir."

"Very good," the captain said. "Now, Colonel, have you discovered a connection between Colonel Hastings and this group?"

"Not yet."

"Answer 'yes' or 'no', please, Colonel."

"No."

"Have you in any way connected Colonel Hastings with any subversive group, with any Communist cell or with any Communist agent?"

"No."

"Have you found any evidence at all in the life of Colonel Hastings to support a charge of disloyalty?"

"No."

"Thank you, Colonel. That will be all."

The colonel took his seat at the rear of the courtroom and Major Wiley of the CID was called and sworn.

Major Wiley was as crisp and self-assured as he had been on Friday night when he and a then-embarrassed Colonel Griswold had knocked on our door. I watched him hostilely. His TWs were crisp from the cleaners, if not the tailors, and his bristly blond hair was fresh cut. I felt a little better when I spotted the nick below his left ear from shaving, but my little glow of pleasure evaporated when he began to testify.

Colonel Krueger asked thoughtfully, "I see from the report that you are the fingerprint expert on the post, Major."

"Yes, sir."

"I have here a photostatic copy of the note found by Sfc. Timothy Sanders in the arms room on the morning in question. Did you fingerprint the original of this note?" And Colonel Krueger handed the copy to the major.

"Yes, sir. On it I found the fingerprints of Colonel Michael Hastings." The major paused for effect. "And the only other fingerprints were those of Sfc. Sanders and Captain Carl Tinsley, both of whom handled the sheet after it was found Wednesday morning."

Captain Brody was on his feet, objecting that the major couldn't prove who had handled the sheet when. Colonel Krueger nodded and said quietly, "Your objection is noted, Captain."

On cross-examination, Captain Brody went after it.

"Major Wiley, did the CID compare this note with the note paper kept in Colonel Hastings' desk?"

The major, his face alert, seemed to sniff around the question before he replied, "Yes, we did so compare the sheet."

"And what were your findings?"

"It was identical to the sheets in Colonel Hastings' office."

"Did you test the top sheet of paper from the stack in Colonel Hastings' office for fingerprints?"

The major frowned. "No, of course not."

"Why not?" Captain Brody asked in a silky voice.

The major shrugged his beautifully-tailored shoulders. "Why should we? What would that prove?"

"Perhaps a man's innocence!" the captain said shortly. "Tell me, Major, if you wished to obtain a sheet of note paper with another man's fingerprints, what would be more likely than the top sheet from the stack of paper in his desk?"

Major Wiley made no reply.

"What do you think, Major?"

The major shrugged again. "I have no thoughts on that subject."

Captain Brody half smiled. "I'm not surprised," he said quietly. Then he continued briskly. "Major, did you also fingerprint the bankbook which was found in Colonel Hastings' quarters?"

"Yes."

"Whose fingerprints are on that bankbook?"

"Several print fragments have been identified as those of bank officials."

Captain Brody waited. He waited a long while and, when the major said nothing more, the captain frowned, "Major, what of Colonel Hastings' fingerprints? Where are they?"

"There are none."

"Major, let me be sure I understand this. There is not one fingerprint of Colonel Michael Hastings on the bankbook which he allegedly received and taped beneath the front drawer of his desk? Not one! Is that correct?"

"Yes, Captain," Major Wiley said grudgingly.

"Thank you, Major."

That was one up for the defense but then sheer weight piled up against us as one by one Colonel Krueger called to the stand the men who had been at Blue Bowl that morning.

The sentries testified that no one, either late on Tuesday or early on Wednesday morning, had passed them carrying a weapon or anything that could conceal a weapon—except Colonel Hastings with his gun case.

The K-9 sergeants testified that no one had come near the compound Tuesday night.

And every man who had been in the command post was called to testify that Dad had his gun case there on Wednesday.

Captain Brody couldn't shake anybody even on the smallest detail. He tried like fury. He made each one admit that the colonel always carried his gun case on Wednesdays, because he went skeet shooting. But he couldn't mitigate the fact that Dad had carried out the only thing that could have held the missing M-18.

I wondered why he didn't go after Sfc. Saunders when he testified so positively that the signature on the note at the arms room was my dad's, but the captain's pursuit of Krovich satisfied me, even though Krovich played it very cagey.

On cross-examination, Captain Brody tried to fish out something helpful to Dad. "Was this man you saw shorter or taller than Colonel Hastings?"

But Krovich was taking care of Krovich. "I just couldn't say, sir," he replied ingenuously. "I only got a glimpse of him. It could have been anybody."

And that's the way it went all morning—the damning testimony, Colonel Krueger's soft-voiced conferences with Captain Andy, Captain Brody's dogged questioning. By the time the Article 32 recessed for lunch, I didn't see how Colonel Krueger could keep from recommending a court-martial.

COLONEL KRUEGER'S INSTRUCTIONS

When the Article 32 reconvened after lunch, Colonel Krueger took his place as quietly and undramatically as before. I wondered what he thought and how he felt about Dad and what he wrote down in the occasional brief notes that he made on the pad of paper in front of him.

"All the government witnesses have been heard," the colonel said. "Captain Brody, have you any witnesses to call for the defense."

"Yes, sir. I will begin by recalling Sfc. Sanders."

"Very well. Sfc. Sanders will take the stand."

Sanders was seated at the back of the courtroom with the rest of the witnesses who had testified. He got to his feet slowly and came down the aisle, his face wary.

When he was seated, Captain Brody walked toward the witness stand and his smooth movement reminded me irresistibly of a cat gliding over grass toward a bird.

"Sergeant, did Colonel Hastings set up a procedure to be followed in the checkout of M-18s?"

"Yes, sir."

"Will you describe it to me?"

The sergeant's broad, heavy face seemed to shrink a little. He hunched his head down between his shoulders and mumbled, "Anybody getting a weapon was supposed to show his identification and sign the log in the cage."

"Could you repeat that louder, Sergeant? I want the investigating officer to be able to hear you."

Sergeant Sanders flushed and said loudly, "Nobody could check out a weapon without showing his ID and signing the log."

Captain Brody leaned forward and demanded sharply, "Why didn't you follow your orders, Sergeant? Why didn't you call the colonel and ask him to sign the log?"

The sergeant's stubby hands gripped the sides of the witness chair. "But the note was signed by the colonel! It was from the colonel!"

"Earlier in this hearing, Sergeant, you examined a photostatic copy of the note that was found on Wednesday morning and you identified the signature as the colonel's. You are familiar with the colonel's signature?"

Sanders' hands relaxed. "Yes, sir. I know the colonel's signature."

"How?"

The sergeant shrugged. "Oh, orders from the colonel and—"

Capt. Brody interrupted. "What signed orders have you ever received from Colonel Hastings? How many?"

Sanders frowned. "I don't know. Maybe four, five times." He raised his head and looked defiant. "But that's not all I've seen his signature. All the orders on the bulletin board and things like that, they're—"

"You mean mimeographed copies of his signature?" Captain Brody asked softly.

Sanders hesitated, then admitted, "Yes, I guess they're mimeographed."

Captain Brody nodded sagely. "So, on the basis of four or five actual signatures and a number of mimeographed signatures, you consider yourself an authority on the colonel's signature. Is that right?"

"I know the colonel's handwriting," the sergeant insisted hotly. "I know it."

"Very good," the captain said easily. He turned back to the defense table, picked up a sheet of paper, and returned to the witness Stand. "Sergeant, I'd like for you to identify this signature," and he handed the paper to Sanders.

The sergeant reached out reluctantly. He stared at the sheet. His eyes flickered from the paper to the captain then back again. An agonized frown creased his forehead.

"Identify it, please, Sergeant," the captain demanded curtly.

Sanders' flushed. "You're trying to make a fool out of me. But I know—"

The cool, dry voice of the investigating officer cut across Sanders' words. "Confine yourself to the question at hand, Sergeant. Can you identify the signature?"

Sanders looked miserably up at the colonel then back at the paper. "It looks like Colonel Hastings' signature," he said finally.

"Does it look like the signature on the note?"

Slowly Sanders nodded. "Yes. It looks just like it."

Capt. Brody reached out for the sheet of paper. When he held it, he looked up at the sergeant and began to smile.

"Thank you, Sergeant Sanders. Thank you very much."

He walked over to the dais and held the paper up to Colonel Krueger. "I would like to offer this sheet of paper for your consideration, sir. It will be basic to my examination of the next witness."

"Very well, Captain."

"Will Mr. Sylvester Renick please come forward to be sworn?" Captain Brody said.

The slender civilian wore a gray suit complete with vest even though the temperature outside was in the nineties, but he didn't look in the least hot or uncomfortable. He looked, in fact, very distinguished.

Colonel Krueger swore him in and Renick identified himself as vice-president of the Liberty Avenue Bank and Trust Company in Stockton.

Mr. Renick spoke quietly but clearly. He had been with the bank ever since 1946. Of late years, the major portion of his time had been spent in investing bank monies.

"I understand you are a writer, also," Captain Brody said.

"Yes, Captain. I am the author of *Ten Famous Forgeries and How They Changed History* and *The Techniques of Forgery*."

Mr. Renick had the undivided attention of the courtroom. The witnesses, now all seated toward the rear, craned to get a better view of him. Even the investigating officer leaned a little farther over the bench and for a fleeting instant his bony face lost its impassivity and reflected intense curiosity.

"When did your interest in forgery begin, sir?" Captain Brody asked.

"In August, nineteen forty-two," the banker responded precisely, "I was assigned to OSS as a second lieutenant. I was trained as a forger. Because I spoke French fluently, I was dropped into Occupied France in nineteen-forty-three, where I spent the rest of the war as liaison with a French resistance group. My primary job was to forge identity papers and other documents."

Mr. Renick described his continuing interest in forgery after his return to civilian life and the books he had written.

Then Captain Brody retrieved from Colonel Krueger the sheet of paper that contained the signature which Sergeant Sanders on the witness stand had identified as my father's. The captain handed the sheet to Mr. Renick.

"Do you recognize this signature, sir?"

"Yes, Captain, I do. It is my work. A forgery of Colonel Michael Hastings' signature." He smiled dryly. "A very simple forgery, really. If you'll notice the jagged uneven script—the colonel's signature is rather easy to do."

Mr. Renick's testimony was the defense's finest hour. Captain Brody had a raft of other witnesses. Men who had gone skeet shooting with Dad on Wednesday testified that he had had his gun case and that it had held his shotgun. Men who had known and served with Dad here and over the world testified as to his character.

Iwo Jima, Corregidor, Wake Island. Pusan, Inchon, Seoul. Da Nang, Hue, and An Khe.

Michael Hastings had been there, he and thousands of other Americans. They didn't do it for money. A Proctor and Gamble trainee makes more. They didn't do it for fun. War is dirt and fear and danger. They did it because they saw it as their job. Their country sent them and so they went.

Michael Hastings came home each time. So many didn't. His first son had not. And today he sat in a courtroom and traced his career, the same career so many Americans had followed, and the room was quiet because the men who listened knew the worth of what they heard.

"Colonel Hastings, you are accused of stealing a new rifle, the M-18, and selling it to a foreign power. Did you do so?"

"No," my father said harshly. Anger flushed his lean tanned face. "I've served my country as best I could all my life. My son died for our country. I'd rather die than betray her."

"Thank you, Colonel," Captain Brody said quietly. "That is all."

Dad looked up and met the inquiring gaze of Colonel Krueger. The investigating officer said quietly, "Colonel, is it your position that you have been deliberately framed?"

"Yes," Dad said forcefully.

"Why should a Soviet agent spend twenty-five thousand dollars to put the blame on you?"

"Only one hypothesis makes sense," Dad said grimly. "It must be worth twenty-five thousand dollars to the Soviets to prevent further investigation."

Colonel Krueger nodded slowly. "Obviously, the thief must be one of the nine men who was in the command post Wednesday morning. It is your position that you are not the man, is that correct?"

"Yes."

Colonel Krueger studied his note pad and tapped it softly with his pencil. Then he looked up and said briskly, "That will be all, Colonel Hastings. Thank you."

Captain Brody stood.

Colonel Krueger said, "Yes, Captain?"

"Sir, the defense is prepared to give its closing argument."

"Defense will have opportunity to speak, Captain, but not at this time," and he looked back down at his pad. Captain Brody was puzzled but he sat down. Then the investigating officer motioned Captain Andy to the bench.

The tall, blond captain bent across the bench and listened intently. They conferred in low voices for a moment, then Captain Andy nodded and resumed his seat.

The investigating officer said quietly, "I wish to recall Colonel Griswold to the stand."

I wondered what Colonel Krueger was up to and what he had asked Captain Andy.

Colonel Griswold's face had a bullish set when he took the stand.

Colonel Krueger, voice even and face as expressionless as usual, didn't mince words. "Colonel, what investigation has the

CID made of the nine other men who were in the command post Wednesday morning?"

"We have interrogated them all."

"Have you investigated their records, checked their backgrounds?"

"No, sir."

Colonel Krueger stared down at his sheet of paper, made a check with his pencil, then pursed his thin mouth and said, "Colonel, the government's case rests on two bases: the bankbook found in the accused's quarters and the gun case carried out of the command post by the accused."

He paused and looked soberly at Colonel Griswold.

"I am not satisfied with the evidence so far presented. I would like for you to conduct a thorough examination of the past histories of all the men present in the command post on four June."

He looked down again at his list, then continued in his even dry voice. "I would further ask that the signatures in question be tested by at least two more handwriting experts and the results be made available to this investigation. I would also like for several tests to be conducted to time the route that Colonel Hastings took from his office to the skeet range and a thorough search of the adjacent area for evidence of any object thrown out or concealed."

Colonel Krueger frowned and said almost conversationally, "If Colonel Hastings' shotgun was in his gun case then he could not have smuggled out the M-18. And half the government's case would be gone."

"Yes, sir," Colonel Griswold replied, his voice tight.

Colonel Krueger picked up his papers and notepad. "The Article 32 will resume at 0900 hours on Thursday, twelve June."

And in the stunned quiet that followed his pronouncement, the colonel pushed back his chair and was through the door behind the dais.

THE IMPERIAL HOTEL

Everything happened at once as the door shut behind Colonel Krueger. Mother was smiling and crying all at the same time. I was shaking Dad's hand and grinning. Captain Brody was saying excitedly, "Colonel, we just may pull it off!" And some of the men who had testified for Dad were trying to reach him.

I saw Major Kelly, a grin on his reddish face, pushing through the crowd toward us. Just ahead of him was Sergeant Elroy. Elroy was frowning, his heavy face creased in thought. He stopped to let a captain by, then started toward us again.

Captain Brody grabbed Dad's arm about that time. "Colonel, I've overlooked a bet. A big bet!"

I jerked around to listen.

"The gun case!" Captain Brody exclaimed. "I'm going to demand that it be submitted to the FBI laboratory for tests. And those tests will prove that the M-18 was never in it! If it had been, some trace of its oils would be left. I don't know why I didn't think about that before."

"That's a great idea!" I said excitedly. Then I was kind of pushed aside as some of Dad's friends made it to him, but they didn't have much of a chance to talk because the MPs were there to take Dad back to the stockade.

For a minute I was furious. The prisoner's time was up. Then I fought down the anger, because things were looking up for us. But it still hurt to see him walking toward the door behind the dais with an MP on either side.

I turned away, looking for Mother, and a few feet from me stood Sergeant Elroy, his hand outstretched as if he would call Dad back, then, still frowning, he looked toward the doors.

I wondered briefly what Elroy wanted. I saw him stop in the hall just past the door and he was talking to somebody. I couldn't see the man he was talking to, just a thick, muscular hand gripping Elroy's arm. Then Elroy nodded hard and the worried frown left his face and he moved out of my sight.

I almost went after him, then I shrugged. I had some thinking to do. I wanted to get Nancy and tell her what had happened and try to figure out how we could use the next two days to help Dad more.

But at seven that night, Nancy and I still hadn't come up with a workable plan to flush the thief, and Nancy was stubbornly insisting that I had to tell her dad how Royce and I figured that the weapon was still in the command post.

"You should have told him Sunday night!"

"Don't you see, Nancy, it won't prove anything to find the rifle! We have to get the man."

"Bart, Daddy wants the guilty man, too. He'll listen to you and help set a trap." She looked at me unhappily. "Is that why you didn't come to see me Sunday? Because you didn't want to tell me what Sergeant Royce said? I waited all day to hear from you. I wanted to go to the Article 32 with you."

I looked down at the top of the kitchen table, avoiding her eyes.

"And tonight you made me promise I wouldn't repeat what you were going to tell me." Her face was troubled. "I won't tell Daddy, Bart. But I think you're making a big mistake. You can't set a trap in Blue Bowl. You can't even get into Blue Bowl. Let Daddy help."

And that's the way it stood when the phone rang. My voice was sharp and irritable when I answered.

A young, uncertain voice asked hesitantly, "Is this the colonel's son?"

"Rodriguez?" I asked quickly.

"Jeez, mister, you asked me to call if I found out anything. And I thought you might want to know that the FBI's going to talk to Elroy. But maybe it don't—"

"The FBI talk to Elroy," I repeated blankly. "Rodriguez, how'd you find that out? What are they going to talk to him about?"

"Jeez, I don't know what about!"

"Then how do you know they're going to talk to him?"

"Well, see, it's like this." And I could picture Rodriguez settling his shoulder against the gray painted wood of the barracks wall and getting ready to tell it to me from the first.

"See," he began, "Me and Elroy walked back from chow together. And Elroy keeps lookin' at his watch and he's kinda excited and jumpy, so I ask him what's the deal, has he got a hot date tonight. He kinda laughs but not much 'cause he's thinkin' about something."

Rodriguez paused for breath. "We were almost to the barracks when he stops and asks if I can keep a secret and I say sure I can. He says he's gonna be big at the Article 32 on Thursday and tonight he's gonna talk to the FBI but he's not supposed to tell anybody."

"Tonight? He's going to talk to the FBI tonight?"

"That's what he said, mister. I asked him if they were coming to the barracks and he says, no, he's supposed to meet 'em at a hotel in Stockton. They rented a room, see, 'cause there's not an FBI office in Stockton."

"When's he going, Rodriguez?"

"He's already left. He's supposed to catch the quarter-'til bus. He left a couple of minutes ago."

"Listen, Rodriguez, thanks a lot. I'm going after him."

I slammed down the phone and turned toward Nancy. "Something's up. The FBI's going to talk to Elroy. I'm going to try and catch up with him and see what's cooking. Mom'll take you home."

"Okay, Bart. Call me when you get home."

And I was halfway up the hall. I skidded to a stop at the living room doorway and called, "Mom, please take Nancy home. I've got to run. She'll explain."

And I was out the door and into the Mustang and backing out into the street. I changed gears and lunged forward. I pushed as far past the speed limit as I dared with an eye out all the way for an MP car.

It wasn't a long way in miles to Pershing but it seemed to take forever before I was passing the NCO housing on one side and the officers' Capeharts on the other.

The light was red at Pershing. I stopped and looked to my left and there, lumbering along, was the bus into Stockton. I checked my watch. Fourteen minutes to eight. Elroy would be on that bus. I could catch him, all right.

When the light changed, I turned left and pretty soon I was riding tail on the bus. I relaxed behind the wheel. When Elroy got off, I'd call to him. So I didn't worry at all as I crept along behind the bus. It stopped and started, belching fumes. It made you believe in air pollution.

Pretty soon we were on the outskirts of Stockton. I lagged back a little. I didn't expect Elroy to get off until we reached the downtown area, which had one nice hotel.

Like a lot of small towns that border Army posts, maybe

like all small towns everywhere, Stockton has its sleazy side: the rinky-tink piano bars, the tattoo parlors, the cheap movie houses. Nevada, which runs east and west, *is* the main artery through this district.

And when the bus stopped at Nevada where it crosses Pershing, Elroy got off, turned to his right, and started up Nevada.

It caught me by surprise. The FBI wouldn't meet anybody on Nevada Street! Maybe Rodriguez had it all wrong. I hesitated, then swung right. When I was even with Elroy, I stopped and called through the open window, "Hey Elroy! Wait a minute. I want to talk to you!"

He half-turned toward the car, frowned darkly, and shook his head. "I can't talk now, Mac. I got business." And he headed on up the sidewalk, walking faster and faster.

And, for the first time, worry threaded through my mind. Elroy had told Rodriguez that he wasn't supposed to tell anybody he was seeing the FBI. That sounded funny. And this was the wrong part of town for the FBI to meet anybody.

I shoved down on the gas and pulled up even with Elroy again. "Wait a minute!" I yelled.

He started to run, his heavy shoulders lowered. He was near the middle of the block now. He threw a swift look over his shoulder then swerved to the right and disappeared into a dingy doorway.

I looked around for a parking place but old shabby cars lined the curb all the way to the end of the block. I was even with the doorway that Elroy had dodged into. Faded gilt letters on the double doors proclaimed THE IMPERIAL HOTEL, ROOMS $4 A NIGHT. Next door was a delicatessen and beyond it gaped the black emptiness of an alley.

I swerved into the alley. It was almost dark now but I could see dimly the rusted trash cans lining the wall. As the sound of the car motor magnified between the walls of the building, an emaciated cat hissed, twisted into a tight circle, and fled in the deepening dusk, up the alley.

The Mustang jolted over cobblestones, but I saw that a used car lot ran up behind the hotel from the next street. I pulled into the lot, slammed out of the car, and started to run. It seemed an age since Elroy had flung that last look over his shoulder and disappeared into the dingy doorway of the Imperial Hotel. How long had it been? A minute? A minute and a half?

I ran toward the mouth of the alley, the clattering of my shoes booming in the quiet darkness. I burst into the Imperial and it was utterly silent. The lobby, a small dark room scarcely big enough for the desk, smelled of old cigars and soiled clothes and, oddly, frying onions. A hand bell sat on the desk. A low-watt lamp burned, but nobody was there. I hesitated for just a second, then started up the stairs to my left.

I moved quietly but fast, taking the old stairs two at a time. At the first floor, I paused and looked up and down the hall. The only sound was the thin crackle of a TV set, seeping from beneath the warped wood of one of the old doors. So I ran for the second flight of stairs.

Halfway up I stopped short.

No light shone down the second floor. I didn't like the thick pool of black that hung above me. In the quiet of the old hotel I heard a slow step, the hesitating step of a man who can't see and isn't sure of what lies ahead.

I heard the scrape of a matchhead, loud in the hot, fetid silence, then the soft tap of a fist against the wood of a door.

The back of my neck prickled. Blood pounded in my ears. I could feel evil. I could sense it and taste it. It was all around me.

It wasn't the FBI that had called Elroy!

"Elroy!" I yelled. "Elroy, get out of here!"

And I pounded up the stairs into the dark.

SIX BLOCKS MORE

When I reached the top of the stairs I saw a brief flash of light down the hall. And I saw Elroy's face, his eyes squinted against the sudden shock of the flashlight's bright glare. The beam of light came from a darkened doorway. Then, with the swiftness of a whip lash, a gloved hand came from behind the light and thrust a knife blade up into Elroy's neck. Elroy grunted and staggered back, and the blood splashed out and down.

The flashlight clicked off and the door slammed shut. The hall was black and quiet again. Only a muffled thud marked Elroy's fall.

I stood there and sickness welled up inside of me and my legs felt like they were made of sponge. Then, stumbling like a blind man, I plunged up the hall.

I stumbled over Elroy. I called his name and clutched his arm but it was flaccid and heavy and I let it drop. My hands were wet. I could feel the warmth of his spreading blood as it welled over his blouse. But it wouldn't flow long. Elroy was dead.

The thick black pall of darkness covered the hall. No light shone. No door opened. No one came.

But I wasn't alone on that floor. A killer listened with me, waiting to see if the doors would open and people would cry out.

No one came. The men who lived in a hotel like this—did they turn in a wine-sodden sleep, then shrug away that strangled call, that muffled thud? Or did they lie and listen, wondering what had happened until their thoughts drifted, because such violence was a part of their lives?

The seconds stretched out and still I knelt by that inert body. Then I heard, infinitesimally small, a click as the knob turned on the door just beyond Elroy's body—the door that had slammed shut after a gloved hand struck out.

Slowly, carefully I began to crawl up the hall. Elroy's body lay between me and the stairs. I could feel the dirt and the dust in the threadbare carpet. It was a special feel—stiff and dry, yet filthy. I wondered if it was the last thing I was going to feel.

The door was opening now. In a breath of time, the killer would see that all lay silent in the hall. And he would switch on that flashlight and pin-point me like a fish to be speared.

I got to my feet then and ran light-footed to the end of the hall. I heard him coming after me as I turned the corner. The opaque window of the fire door at the end of the hall glimmered like a lighthouse beacon, spelling the way to life—if it wasn't locked.

I reached it and pulled with hands as strong as terror can make them. The light of the flash spilled around me, but the door was opening and I was plunging out onto the fire escape when he threw the knife.

The knife stung as it slashed past my arm and I could feel blood again and it was warm and it was mine, but I was clambering down the fire escape and I wasn't dead.

At the first flight landing I swung like a monkey and dropped to the alleyway, and then I leaned against the wall to drag huge gulps of air into my lungs because the rungs above me were quiet.

The killer wasn't going to play without his knife.

And then I did a stupid thing. I stumbled directly to the Mustang where it was parked only fifteen feet from the back of the hotel. I climbed in and locked the doors. My arm hurt and the blood was scudding down and dripping off my hand. I pulled out my handkerchief and wadded it inside my sleeve.

I sat there for a long minute or two and tried to think. I had to get the cops, but I didn't know where the police station was. And I was close to the post. And Elroy was an Army man.

Maybe I just wanted to go back to my own territory like a wounded animal crawling home. I switched on the key and gunned the motor. I headed for the post.

I would go directly to General Loring. That was the quickest, the best thing to do. He could get the law there in an instant. And now he would listen to me because Elroy's murder was proof that the Blue Bowl business wasn't finished yet.

And I had the beginnings of a plan.

I drove carefully because I had to concentrate to drive at all. My arm hurt more every minute. It seemed a long time before I stopped to show my pass to the sentry at the post gates. He flicked his light into my face but he didn't see my arm.

The three-mile stretch through the pine trees was interminable. I had a great feeling of relief when I swung off Pershing onto Grant. I was hanging onto the steering wheel at that point, but I knew it wasn't far now. Past the housing and the officers' club and the empty stretch along the Kanakee, then the old houses, and, finally, the house on the hill, the commanding general's quarters.

The little globular reflecting lights blinked to life on the railing that marked the edge of the bluff and the long drop to the Kanakee River. They glowed like fiery coals in the wash of my headlights. I picked up speed a little. Not far now. I was into the deserted stretch between the officer's club and the old houses for senior officers.

The car behind me—I'd noticed its lights a while back—suddenly spurted out to pass me. Instinctively I eased up on the accelerator. The car crowded close and I thought he was crazy. Then I knew he wasn't.

The bluff curved back to the left here. He was running me off the road. I jammed on the brakes and the Mustang's rear slid to the right. His car, bigger and heavier, crashed into the Mustang and it was like the crash cars at the amusement park. I was slammed hard against the door and everything happened at once. The Mustang hurtled through the railing and flipped over and I was thrown out. I slammed hard into some scrub brush, crashed through it, and, halfway down the bluff, brought up against the trunk of a tree.

I heard the Mustang crash into the side of the bluff below me. Then an explosion boomed and fire flashed and the flaming car rolled on to drop into the deep waters of the Kanakee.

I hurt all over. My body trembled uncontrollably—until I saw the flashlight beam flicker over the edge of the bluff.

The killer was making sure. I turned my face into the dirt and lay as still as the ground itself. The snaking beam raked up and down the bluff. But, finally, the light went off.

I didn't try to move. The trembling had come back and the awareness of pain. But, most of all, I wasn't going to underestimate the killer again.

He hadn't given up when he didn't get me at the hotel. Now, pain-fuddled as I was, I understood. He had to kill me or the frame around my dad would begin to crumble. If I got back with the word that Elroy had thought he was meeting the FBI, then the fat was in the fire. And the killer had to assume that I knew this—or why would I have been at the hotel at all?

I hoped Rodriguez was keeping his mouth shut. Because death was very close to him.

It was very quiet. Occasionally a car passed above me on Grant. I could hear the whine of its wheels. Night creatures rustled in the thick tufts of weeds nearby.

I don't know how long I'd been there when the flashlight flicked on again and swept swiftly up and down the bluff. Clever man. Dangerous man.

And when it was gone again, I waited yet a while longer. I lay there and thought about Elroy. Poor dumb Elroy who was so out of place in an office. He shouldn't have died in the corridor of a cheap hotel. He should have died in the field, where he belonged.

And I was pretty sure I knew why Elroy had died. He had tried to talk to my dad after the Article 32. And the last thing Colonel Krueger had emphasized was that the government's case was zilch if anyone had seen my dad's gun in the gun case.

During the Article 32 would have been the first time Elroy would have heard about the gun case. All he knew was that the colonel was in trouble because the M-18 was gone. And today he had heard the government accuse Dad of carrying the M-18 out in his gun case.

But Elroy must have known that couldn't be true. I thought I knew what had happened. Elroy had spent some time alone in Dad's office that Wednesday morning—and Elroy loved guns. What would be more natural than for him to take a look into the gun case? And Elroy couldn't be confused about an M-18 and a shotgun. His testimony could have knocked the frame from here to Moscow and the search would begin, the fine-tooth search for the traitor among the nine.

So Elroy had tried to talk to Dad but the MPs had taken Dad off before he reached him. Someone in that courtroom had seen Elroy make that attempt. But who? And I had seen Elroy talking to somebody in the hall. I tried to picture that strong muscular hand clamped on Elroy's arm, but I couldn't match it to a body.

I faded in and out as I lay there. One minute everything would be clear in my mind and then it would grow far away and funny like a dream. But I held onto my plan, the one I had started to General Loring with, because it had grown clearer and more distinct and I could see a real chance now—if I could just make it to General Loring.

The sound of "Taps" cut sharply across the night and I knew it was eleven. I listened to the sad, lonely notes rise and fall, and when it was quiet I tried to move.

Sweat beaded my face. My back ached like a sledgehammer had caught me across the kidneys. I managed to get up on my hands and knees. My left wrist throbbed, my legs were scratched, but everything seemed in working order.

Scrub brush and stunted trees clung to the side of the bluff. Clawing my way through the scrub, I reached a faint path that followed the curve of the bluff. It was slippery, dry and pebble-strewn, but it couldn't be seen from above. I stumbled along the path, tripping now and then over up-thrust roots and once I fell full-face over a fallen tree branch and I lay there for a long time before I could get up again.

The pale moonlight distorted the path. It was like trying to walk in one of those spook houses that have just enough luminescent paint to throw everything out of kilter.

I ran out of path when the bluff steepened to sheer cliff. I could hear the rolling waters of the Kanakee roaring below me. I had almost forgotten what I was trying to do and why. I stood there stupidly, my puffy face squeezed tight, trying to think.

The general. I had to get to the general. I looked up and I

could see lights and I realized I had scrabbled along the bluff to the point where the old quarters began.

I started up. The gradient was fairly easy until I was almost to the top, when the bluff jutted sharply up the last few feet.

I pulled myself up, slowly, achingly, from one scrub brush to the next. A couple of feet from the top, a stunted tree clung to its hold on the now sheer face. I grabbed it and pulled up until I hung over that scraggly tree like a rope over a chock. Then bracing with my right hand, I got one knee up and with a final lunge pushed up over the top. I flopped over like a dead man, but I struggled up on my hands and knees, then made it to my feet.

The street lay quiet and serene. Light splashed down from the street lamps in bright patches. Occasional lights shone in the old two-story houses. Halfway up the street was our house. But I didn't even look at it as I passed.

The general. I had to get to the general. It was six long blocks to General Loring's quarters. Six long stumbling blocks that I couldn't remember when I'd finished them.

When I crunched up the circular graveled drive, I was almost past thought. I fell down twice and there was nothing in my way. I reached the front door and pressed my finger against the bell. I leaned against the screen and, slowly, began to slide down. But I kept my finger on the buzzer as I fell.

A REPORT TO MAKE

"Hush, Nancy. He's not dead. He's coming around. Get some more water, then call the hospital. I want a doctor here immediately."

"Oh Daddy, his face! And his arm! And his clothes are all torn. He's—"

"Do as I say," the general said sharply. "I don't think he's seriously injured. Heartbeat steady. No massive blood loss."

I heard it all dimly and I struggled to sit up. A strong hand gently pushed me back into the softness of the cushions. I opened my eyes and pushed away the restraining hand and tried again to sit up.

"General, Elroy's dead! They've killed Elroy!" My voice was hoarse and weak but he heard. He pulled me up and helped me sit back against the end of the couch.

"Who killed him? When?"

Nancy burst back into the living room and Mrs. Loring was at her heels. "We've called the hospital," Mrs. Loring said.

Nancy burst out, "Daddy, don't let him talk! He's hurt!"

The general brusquely waved her away. "He's ambulatory," he said crisply. "And he has a report to make."

Nancy was crying, the tears running in silent streaks down

her face, and it looked all wrong because she was so pretty in a pale-blue summer robe.

I didn't think then to be surprised that the general knew immediately who Elroy was. The general ran a troop post of ten thousand men, but he knew who Elroy was because that was one of the names that figured in the M-18 disappearance. His immediate recognition showed what it took to be a general.

I told it all to him, starting with the phone call from Rodriguez, the quick trip after the bus, the darkened landing in the Imperial Hotel, the blood flowing over Elroy's blouse, and the click of the doorknob, my escape and the car that had spurted around me on Grant Avenue.

It had all taken so long to happen but I gave it to him in five minutes or less. He reached out for the phone the minute I finished, and I said quickly, "What are you going to do, sir?"

"Call the Stockton police first. Tell them what you've reported, then call out the MPs and the CID."

"Don't use my name, sir. Don't."

His hand rested on the receiver. His face darkened and he asked angrily, "What the devil do you mean, Bart? Of course I have to use your name. You have to tell the police what happened, man!"

"Wait, sir, please. Don't you see, the killer thinks I'm dead. That means we can trap him."

His hand slid away from the receiver. "I don't see what you mean. At all."

I pulled up straighter against the soft cushions of the divan. Sweat beaded my face as one word tumbled over another. If I couldn't sell it to the general, Dad was lost. They'd never catch the killer, never prove Elroy's death had anything to do with the missing M-18. They'd just say Elroy made it up about going to the FBI, that it was one of those casual knifings in a cheap part of town.

I laid it all out before the general: how Sergeant Royce and I figured the weapon was still in the command post; how Colonel Krueger said there wasn't any case if anyone had seen inside the gun case; and how Elroy had been in Dad's office and how he loved guns.

". . . and Elroy tried to get to Dad right after Colonel Krueger said that. Then he must have told the wrong man, because he left the barracks convinced he was going to be the star witness at the 32. And it was phony. It was to make sure he never told anyone ever what he'd seen in the gun case!"

"If the M-18's in the command post, I'll have it found. Now." And he picked up the receiver.

"Sir!"

A hard line ridged his jaw. "What?"

"Don't you see, sir, finding the gun won't catch the killer. You want to catch him, don't you?"

"I want the rifle. I want the man who took it. I want the killer. You say they're the same. Then every second I waste talking to you gives him longer to cover his tracks." He picked up the telephone receiver and started to dial.

"They're already covered for tonight," I said desperately. "You won't find him by calling the Stockton cops. And Elroy's not in a hurry for anything anymore. But I know how you can get the killer and the M-18!"

His broad fingers hesitated as he dialed the third digit. Then quietly he depressed the cradle bar and looked long at me.

"All right, Bart, tell me why you don't want the Stockton police to know you were at the Imperial Hotel, and tell me how we can trap the killer."

And then the doorbell rang. Mrs. Loring answered it and

let in a captain with the medical caduceus on his blouse and a satchel in his hand. He started right for me. I guess I looked pretty much like a patient.

He stopped short when he saw the general and said breathlessly, “Sorry to be held up, sir. A patient in surgery, but I’ll get right to work.”

The general held up his hand. “Captain, do you have any patients needing your immediate care at the hospital?”

The captain looked puzzled, but his was not to reason why when a general inquired. “No, sir, not right now.”

“Will the hospital call here if an emergency arrives?”

“Yes, sir.”

“Then go back to the kitchen. My daughter will fix you a cup of coffee. I must hear the rest of this man’s report before he is treated.”

“Daddy!” Nancy exploded. “Bart needs—”

“Bart will survive,” the general said crisply. “Do as I order.”

And she did. The captain didn’t hesitate. His still not to question. Mrs. Loring led the way.

“Nancy, close the door as you leave,” her father said quietly. And as the door swung to behind them, he nodded to me. “Be quick.”

“The police mustn’t know I was at the hotel, because then the killer will learn that I’m alive. And the most important thing of all is for him to believe I’m dead. Because he’ll think he’s completely safe. There’s nothing left to trip him up.”

The general’s eyes narrowed. “So he thinks you’re dead. What then?”

“Then he’ll fall for the trap. I’ve got a plan and I know it will work! You’re the general, you can order darn near anything you please, so you can fix it.”

“Fix what?” he asked sharply.

"If the M-18 is hidden in the command post and the killer finds out the command post is going to be blown up, he'll break his neck trying to get the M-18 out, right? And you can catch the killer and get the weapon back all at the same time."

General Loring frowned. "Why should Blue Bowl command post be blown up?"

I smiled. He was listening, really listening. "Because you order it as part of a training exercise. It's an old ramshackle farmhouse. Nobody would think twice about it if you decided to use it for a target in a rocket attack."

I started to push up straighter with my left hand then gave a grunt as pain exploded in my wrist. When the mist cleared away, I said doggedly, "We can do it, sir. We can outfox the killer. Tomorrow is Tuesday. The first thing in the morning, you can notify Major Kelly that the M-18 testing exercise is being postponed and the M-18s removed because the command post is going to be blown up in a rocket launcher demonstration. And you can have the post crawling with CID while the move is made so the killer won't try anything then. And the sentries will still be checking everything out of the command post like they were Customs inspectors."

"If there are CID men everywhere while the command post files and materials are being packed, won't it tip off the killer?"

"You can substitute CID men for the regular Transportation people. Then late in the afternoon, when the move is complete, you can dismiss the sentries and have the notices posted that Blue Bowl command post will be bombed at 0800 Wednesday morning—and what do you bet our pal creeps into the command post sometime Tuesday night?"

The general walked slowly up and down the living room, his head bent in thought. Finally he stopped by the couch.

"If the M-18's there, it ought to work." He smiled a coldly-satisfied smile. "He'll bite. He'll have to bite."

He strode to the phone. I waited, holding my breath, but it was all right. I had sold the general.

He spoke crisply into the phone. "Colonel Griswold? Sorry to bother you this late, but I'd like you to come over here immediately."

The call made, he gestured to me to come over to the phone. I pushed up from the couch, then held onto the arm, fighting off dizziness.

"Sorry, Bart. Forgot for a minute. Sit down."

I sat down heavily, gritting my teeth. Everything hurt.

The general was carrying the phone over to the couch.

"Pull yourself together, boy. You'll get to rest pretty soon now. I want you to call your mother, assure her you're all right, then let me speak to her."

With fingers that felt thick and heavy and swollen, I picked up the receiver and carefully dialed.

Mother answered on the first ring, her voice sharp and anxious, "Colonel Hastings' quarters, Mrs. Hastings speaking."

"Mother, it's me, Bart."

"Oh, Bart, thank God!" And then quickly, angrily she said, "Where are you? Do you realize it's after midnight! Where have you been?"

"Mom, I've had quite a night, but I'm fine, just fine. I'm at General Loring's home. I'm going to put him on the phone. He wants to talk to you."

I handed the phone to the general and sank back against the couch. The sweat was running down my face and I felt lousy.

"Celia, this is Martin. I know you've been worried about Bart and that's what I've called about. I'm going to ask you to help him and help me clear Mike. And it's going to take some tough duty on your part."

He smiled at her response. "That's a girl. Bart's had a hard night. The traitor who stole the gun killed one of Mike's EMs tonight and Bart stumbled on the scene. He got away but the killer came after him and crowded his car off Grant into the Kanakee. Bart was thrown free."

He waited a moment until Mother finished speaking, then said very clearly, "The important point, Celia, is that the killer thinks Bart is dead—and we want him to go right on thinking that. For one thing, it keeps Bart safe, and for another, it makes the killer feel completely secure. As far as he knows, everybody who could upset the applecart is out of the way. And while he's feeling all safe and cozy, we're going to prepare a trap for him. One your son figured out, as a matter of fact. If everything goes right, Celia, Bart and Mike will both be home safe and sound on Wednesday morning,"

Mother must have spoken pretty sharply, because the general answered quickly. "No, Celia, there's no danger to Bart in it, none at all. Not if you do your part right. I want you to call the provost marshal's and explain, in a very upset fashion, that Bart isn't home, you don't know where he is. Ask them to hunt for him. Probably the broken guardrail won't be noticed until morning and then it will take some time to set up dragging operations. But, whomever you see, I don't care who it is, you play the part of a terribly worried mother. And that's all there is to it."

He listened for a moment, then said, "Sure. Here he is."

He handed the phone back to me. Mother's voice was strained and worried. "Bart, are you really all right?"

"Sure, Mom. Right as rain. It was a pretty bad night but everything's great now. Dad's going to be okay, Mom. I just know it's going to work out."

"All right, Bart," she said and her voice almost managed not to waver. She was a real Army wife. But then she said so fast and low that I almost couldn't hear, "Please, Bart, take care. You are my only son now."

"Sure, Mom. I will. I promise."

But as I handed the phone back to the general, I found it hard to breathe because Mom knew as well as I that some promises can't be kept. When she'd said goodbye to Kyle, she'd pled, "Please, son, take care."

But Kyle was dead. So far my luck had ridden high. Twice now the killer had tried to get me and twice I'd escaped. Third time's the charm. I wondered as I slumped there for whom the charm would work, third time out.

The general was back at the phone but this time he rang the kitchen extension. "Nancy? Time for that medic to get to work. I'm carrying Bart up to Tommy's room."

He put down the phone and stepped over to the couch. I roused and said in a blurred voice, "That's all right, sir, I can—"

"Quiet, son. You've done more than enough tonight," and he picked me up like I weighed no more than a kitten, even though I played halfback on the freshman squad. But I was too tired to argue.

Everything was pretty fuzzy when he laid me gently down on a bed in Tommy's old room. The doctor began to get my clothes off and I remember calling out, "General, sir, don't forget Rodriguez. If he talks. . . ."

"Don't worry," his crisp voice said. "I won't forget Rodriguez."

And finally the doctor was through. My wrist and arm were bandaged and my head, too. I hadn't even known that I'd gashed it in my tumble from the car. My ribs were taped and there were enough patches on me to match a poor boy's inner tube. But the doctor thought my back was okay, probably just wrenched. He slapped me on the shoulder and said in a horribly jolly voice, "Looks like you'll live to fight another day."

I managed a weak grin, but right then I didn't feel like I'd live until he got out of the room.

"One parting shot," he said happily, and he jabbed me in the arm with a hypodermic. He was a real comic. The shot was the whammo kind. I could feel myself falling into sleep like a dive from the top of a skyscraper.

"I've got to get up early. . . ." and my mind ran out of words and I was deep, deep down in thick white folds of sleep.

THE STAIRS CREAK

The early morning sun poured into the breakfast room at the Loring's. I could hear birds chirping and feel the fresh, early morning air through the open window.

It was going to be a beautiful day. And as I listened to the general, I felt sure it was going to be a successful day. We were going to get the killer. We were going to get him so tight he'd never wiggle free. It was half past six. For five hours' sleep, I felt pretty good. It hadn't been so great at first. Sore muscles are pretty bad when you wake up but every minute helped and now I didn't feel any worse than after a tough football game except for the ribs and a dull ache in my head. I could put up with those.

"So you see," the general concluded briskly, "it's all laid on."

And it was. I ticked it off in my mind. In about two hours, Major Kelly would get the word at his office to gear up for the immediate removal of the M-18s and transfer of all command post files and furniture to high security storage until further notice.

And the word would get around quickly that the general had ordered Ninth Infantry Group, Battery Three to destroy the command post at 0800 Wednesday morning in a pinpoint rocket-launcher demonstration to impress some visiting congressmen.

The killer should fall for it. And he would be forced to make his move that night. He couldn't get the rifle out of the compound while the sentries were on duty. He would have to wait until the move was complete. And when it was complete, he would have to go along with the other personnel to brigade HQ. Sometime after five o'clock that afternoon and before eight o'clock the next morning, he would have to get the M-18.

"You didn't miss a thing," I said after a minute.

General Loring looked at me from under his thick gray eyebrows and his brown eyes glinted. "I tried not to," he said dryly.

I flushed. "I'm sorry, sir. I didn't mean to sound smart."

He laughed. "At ease, son. My joke. Feel like I've earned one."

I asked with sudden suspicion, "When did you get to bed, sir?"

"Haven't yet," he said easily. "I'll catch a nap at the office. One prerogative of being a general is having a couch in your office. But I don't even feel tired. Always enjoyed night exercises."

And he didn't look tired. He looked crisp and alert and competent. I felt even better about the day.

He picked up his coffee mug, drained what was left, and pushed back his chair. "Speaking of offices, I think I'll get on over there. Make a last-minute review."

"Sir," I said anxiously, "can I please be one of the men who closes in on the command post tonight?"

His eyes glinted again. "I wondered when you were going to ask to see action." His face sobered. "And I wondered what I was going to say when you did." He looked me over and I tried to sit easily in the chair, like every muscle didn't hurt. Slowly, he shook his head. "I know you want to be in on the finish, but you aren't in any shape to move over that rough country and not make any more noise than a shadow."

His eyes were understanding but his headshake firm. "No, Bart. This is an Army maneuver. I spent some time last night deciding exactly what I was going to do with you today. Mrs. Loring's sewing circle meets here today. I could have had her cancel it, but I don't want to raise eyebrows about anything. And we have to keep you completely under cover. So when I was trying to think of a spot in the post where no one goes, I remembered the attic out at the Blue Bowl command post."

I started to smile.

"Now it's going to make a long day for you." he cautioned. "I've arranged with Sgt. Royce to smuggle you in. He'll be here in about fifteen minutes. I decided he was the only man out there we could trust, because he'd never even have hinted the rifle was there if he were the killer. Once there you'll have to be absolutely quiet, but tonight, after our man is trapped, you can come out. So you'll be on the spot even if you can't be in on the action."

"Thank you, sir," I said quietly.

"Nancy's fixed a basket for you." He pointed to a brown wicker basket that sat on the bright-yellow kitchen counter. He grinned. "I think she misunderstood and thought you were off to the Arctic for a week. Anyway, you can spend the day eating—provided you do it quietly."

He stood then. "Tommy's things fit you all right?" he asked suddenly, and his voice was gruff and pain flickered in his eyes.

"Yes, sir. Perfectly, sir."

"He was a good officer," his father said softly. His mouth tightened and he continued abruptly, "Anyway, you can move around some this afternoon when everybody's gone. But be on your toes from five o'clock on."

It was a piece of cake getting into the command post. Sgt. Royce showed up at the general's with a three-quarter-ton truck, stowed me in the back, and rumbled directly to the Blue Bowl.

The sentries checked him past, but they didn't look in the truck. Why should they? The truck was going in, not coming out.

He backed the truck up to the rear door of the farmhouse. I slipped out and in the door and a minute later I was up in the attic.

The attic stretched the width of the house. It was dusty and quiet but light streamed cheerfully in from a window at the side. An old couch, its cushions sagging, sat by the window. A broken kitchen chair and old bathtub were the only other things up there.

Sergeant Royce helped me pull the couch out a little from the window. He had brought along a couple of Army blankets and we laid these behind the couch and I had a nice hidden resting place.

"If anybody comes, which isn't likely, you can crawl back behind the couch. It should work. And the stairs creak coming up here. So you're all right. Just keep an ear peeled."

He stopped at the door. "Take it easy. I'll see you tonight. I'm one of the men the general picked to cover the command post."

"See you later, then," I said happily. "And thanks, Sergeant."

After he was gone, I wandered around for a while. It was still early, not quite seven yet. I settled down on the couch finally and pulled the thermos out of the wicker basket. I dug down and found four blueberry muffins wrapped in a white napkin. The muffins were still warm. I smiled and poured a cup of coffee from the thermos and drank it and ate all four muffins.

By that time, the command post personnel were beginning to arrive. Car doors slammed and I heard the movement of men on the stairs and in the offices below. It was time to take cover—just in case.

I crawled behind the sofa and lay down on the blankets and looked up at the sharply peaked roof of the attic. But I wasn't seeing the roof—I was seeing faces.

Who would come tonight?

Major Kelly, with his cold, gray eyes and good-humored smile? A jolly, plump, quick-witted man. Was he the one?

Or would it be Captain Tinsley, his bony face thrust forward, his light, mad eyes glittering with triumph?

Or it might be Lieutenant Fagin, dropping his colorless robot-like personality and turning up as a very different kind of man.

It might be Sergeant Sanders. Sergeants don't make much money. Maybe this one had been bought and paid for.

Who would slip quietly across the rugged countryside to Blue Bowl HQ?

Krovich? He was a weasel, ever eager to play the angles, to fix it for Number One. It might be Krovich.

Or it could be the likeable Rodriguez or the lean and casual Schwartz.

I only knew for sure that it wouldn't be Elroy or Sergeant Royce.

But I didn't know who would come tonight.

The faces swirled in my mind, so many men, so many different kinds of men.

I drifted into an uneasy sleep, hearing first one and then another talk, watching their faces in my dream. Then I sank into a deep and heavy sleep. I slept like a dead man for four hours. When I started to wake, it was like climbing out of a molasses bog. When I managed to peer muzzily around, I couldn't figure out for a minute where I was or why I felt so sore or what the banging and thumping noises below could be. And then it all came back and I realized that the noises that had wakened me meant the move was under way. The command post was being stripped.

I drank some coffee and felt more human. Then I eased out from behind the sofa and tiptoed over to the side window and looked out. The farmyard was a scene of frenzied activity, men carrying boxes, chairs and desks to the waiting trucks.

My watch showed it was ten minutes after eleven. I had a lot of hours yet to pass. I wondered why I hadn't thought to bring a book or a puzzle or something. But I hadn't. I ate lunch, a sardine-and-cream-cheese sandwich, one of my favorites, and drank some more coffee. But that only took five minutes.

Then I was left alone with my thoughts and nothing to do but think them. It was the first time since Friday night that I had not been running or fighting or searching.

Friday night. The mean-faced mob in Stockton Square. Father Rosser falling under the fists of a yelling mountain of a man. And me. All ready to go home and tell Dad his world was a lie. Tell him that Kyle died half a world away only because the American colonialists were on the wrong side of a civil war.

I sat with my back against the rough wood of the attic and stared emptily across the dim attic.

Friday night and this was Tuesday, and in a way everything had changed and in another nothing had.

The war still raged half a world away. Men like Kyle and Tommy were still dying half a world away. And men were still hating right here at home like the screaming mob that met us in Stockton Square.

But I had changed. I still thought it was a bad war. I still thought a man should march against it if he wanted to. But I didn't buy the radicals' approach anymore, because the same argument that justifies smashing up a Selective Service office can be used by those right-wingers to justify smashing Father Rosser down on the ground.

You can't have it both ways. They tell you you can't have your cake and eat it, too. And I was beginning to see what they meant. Just because you believed something to be right didn't mean you could do anything in the world to have your way—not if you really wanted to keep a democracy.

It could be an awful lot worse than it was. And that wasn't what I wanted. I wanted it to be better.

I couldn't stand by and see the wrongs and not do anything. The starving kids in the Appalachians, the millionaires who pay no taxes, the thousand and one bars a comfortable white society has erected against its black people.

But I didn't know where that left somebody like me. The riots had changed things. The student battle against the war had dumped one president—and might dump another if Vietnam didn't end. But one day there might be one riot too many. And what then?

What was it Father Rosser had said? No easy answers, that was it. No easy answers anywhere—for me or anybody else.

I was so absorbed I didn't notice the sound until the stairs creaked the second time. I frowned and listened and a third creak came.

Somebody was coming up the stairs to the attic!

THE MAN NOBODY SEES

I stuffed the scraps of my lunch and the thermos back into the basket and picked it up and ran, all in one swift movement. I was back in my hole, but just barely, when the door opened and someone walked in. The door clicked shut. Carefully, I turned myself around and eased to the end of the sofa and peered out.

On the floor near the door, his back to me, knelt a man in blue denims, the kind that have straps over the shoulders. Beside him sat a huge gray metal toolbox.

I relaxed. The maintenance man. Something to do with the move, probably. The general was certainly going in for realistic details.

Then the man looked over his shoulder toward the door and I stopped breathing. I literally couldn't drag air into my lungs for a long moment.

I knew that face. God, I'd never forget that face. Thin and pointed with curly black hair. Deep lines furrowed the cheeks to the tight-drawn mouth. The last time I'd seen that mouth it had been stretched wide. He'd been screaming and yelling and leading the mob into the marchers in Stockton Square.

I watched with the same crawling horror that I'd watch the flat head of a water moccasin move in a pond where I was swimming.

He stared at the door for a long moment, then turned back to work. He was unscrewing part of the floor. I watched and I knew that I had been a fool!

Who can move about unnoticed on an Army post? Who's the man nobody sees? How easy it must have been for him to make up an order to check the wiring in the older quarters. And it had been the work of seconds to tape that all-important bankbook to the underside of the center drawer in Dad's desk.

I wondered if his tight-drawn mouth had loosened in a smile when the drawer was safely shoved home and another strand complete in the web that was to enmesh Colonel Hastings.

And the M-18! How he'd fooled us. No one had thought about the maintenance man, because he was in the command post on Tuesday morning before the shipment arrived. Yes, he was here preparing the hiding place for the gun to be stolen.

I wondered how he had managed to get the M-18? Had he bribed his way past a sentry? Or had he somehow managed to evade the dog teams on Tuesday night?

I didn't know. I only knew that now he was here. I watched him put down a second screw and methodically switch the screwdriver to the other end of the floorboard. It wouldn't be long now and he'd have the rifle out.

And nobody outside to catch him. Tonight men would slip through the dark woods as silently as wraiths, but they would come in vain.

Now was the moment, now the danger. And I was the only one there.

My muscles tensed. If I rushed him. . . . I looked at his back. He was thin but wiry and he held a screwdriver in his hand—the same hand that had plunged a knife into Elroy's throat.

If I jumped him, I was a dead man. I knew it.

Maybe I could rush him and yell for help at the same time.

I listened then, listened for the sounds of men moving about below, for the noise of feet on the old wooden stairs, for the brusque commands of the Transportation sergeants.

The thick, sleepy quiet of a hot summer afternoon covered the farmhouse like a shroud.

I heard the tiny click as the killer dropped the third screw on the wooden floor—and nothing more.

The move was over. The men were gone and the trucks and the files and the M-18s—all save one. Sweat trickled into my eyes and stung. And the sentries would be gone, too. No one to stop him.

Only me. And I was having trouble breathing. My throat was closed as tight and hard as if somebody had jammed a pipe down it. And the sweat was all over me now, running off my face, drenching my shirt and pants.

The last screw clicked onto the floor. He lifted up the board and the M-18 was out. Quickly, expertly, he broke it down. Opening up his toolbox, he fit the pieces into it. He snapped the tool case shut.

I took a deep breath and got ready to push the sofa out and jump—and he was on his feet and moving like a cat to the door and through it.

I hadn't been fast enough. I squeezed out from behind the sofa and ran to the door. He was already at the bottom of the narrow flight that led down from the attic to a door that opened on the second floor. He stood, his back to me, and peered out of the narrowly opened door.

His left hand held the tool case. His right hand abruptly plunged into a big side pocket of the overalls and he pulled out a revolver.

I stood rigidly at the top of the attic stairs. Had he heard me? If he looked back, he would see me at once.

Why had he stopped? What had he seen?

Then I heard the cheery young voice. "Jeez, sergeant. I don't see nothin' else we can cart out of here." There was a vigorous scruffing sound. "And why'd you wanna go in that cellar anyway? I got spider webs in my ears! Nobody's been down there since that smart farmer sold it to Uncle."

Sergeant Royce laughed. "Probably make you hear better, Rodriguez. But I'll tell you, the captain said make a last check. And when I check, I check it all."

"Oh, oh, Sergeant, you're gonna get KP. You forgot about the attic!"

Royce hesitated for only a split second, then said easily, "I was up there the other day. Nothing but junk."

Their voices were growing fainter. They must be almost to the front door. I wanted to yell. But if I yelled, he and Rodriguez would be sitting ducks for a desperate and dangerous man. The killer hadn't pulled the gun for exercise. He was prepared to shoot.

So I didn't yell. And the front door slammed behind Royce and Rodriguez.

The wiry man started to pocket the gun, then he stopped. The front door was opening again and voices sounded in the hall.

"No, Sergeant, no need for you to stay. Seem to have mislaid my briefcase, that's all. You and Rodriguez get on back."

"Okay, Major, if you're sure we can't help hunt for it."

"No need, no need," came the brisk well-remembered voice.

Again the front door slammed shut and Major Kelly's quick footsteps clipped across the hall floor and up the stairs. The killer peered through the partly opened door from the attic flight and pocketed his gun.

The major reached the second floor and turned down the hallway toward the command post offices, empty now. Outside a jeep roared to life, Rodriguez and Royce leaving.

As the sound of the jeep faded away, the killer pushed open the door, looked briefly down the hall, then headed for the stairs to the first floor. I crept quietly along. When I reached the bottom of the attic stairs, I could hear his soft footfalls in the first-floor hall, crossing to the front door.

Now every second counted. Major Kelly hadn't reached the command post on foot and I was sure he would be every bit as tough as Royce in a fight. I ran lightly up the hall. Where was he?

And then he stepped into the doorway of the main office and for a split second he looked absolutely shocked.

"Major," I said softly. "I don't have time to explain but you've got to believe me. The missing M-18 is on its way out of here right this minute. The traitor's a maintenance man. I saw him get the rifle out of a hiding place in the attic just a few minutes ago." I gripped his arm. "You've got a car?"

"Truck," he answered automatically.

"Then come on. We'll follow him and when we spot him, I can stay and watch to see he doesn't get away and you can get the MPs."

Without a word, he turned and started for the stairs, moving fast but not making a sound. As I followed, I knew I hadn't underestimated Major Kelly. He was a man for action. The words could come later.

As we got downstairs, the maintenance man's panel truck was sputtering to life. Major Kelly turned toward the back door. I reached for his sleeve, but he kept on moving. "His truck's out back. Saw it when I parked mine. Come on."

We waited until the panel truck revved up and had driven around the corner of the farmhouse, then we tumbled out the back door. A three-quarter-ton truck waited.

Major Kelly motioned me into the cab. "Borrowed it from Transportation when I missed my briefcase," he explained. "But it wasn't here. Must've mislaid it in all the mess of moving. Can't imagine why the general wanted to pull a surprise stunt like this."

"It's all part of the plan," I said as I watched tensely out the windshield. The panel truck was picking up speed as it passed by the now empty sentry box.

The big truck slowed a little. "Part of the plan?" the major asked.

"Yeah. We had it all figured out that the rifle must be hidden in the command post, so the general set it up to look like the post was going to be blown to splinters. We only had one thing wrong. The man who stole the rifle wasn't part of the command post. It was the maintenance man."

The truck turned heavily onto the winding dirt road that led out of Blue Bowl. Thick-leaved branches met overhead and in the cool tunnel the heavy truck lumbered over the road.

"Can't we go faster?" I urged. "If we lose him, well lose everything."

"He's right ahead," the major said. "But we don't want to ram his tailgate. Don't worry. We won't lose him." He paused. "Why didn't the CID nab him at the command post?"

"Because we didn't think anybody would make a try for the rifle until tonight. The CID was supposed to surround the post after dark."

The major picked up speed. "So what were you doing in the command post?"

"I had to stay hidden." I told him why. "And the general knew I wanted to be in on the kill so Sergeant Royce smuggled me in early this morning."

"So you're the only one who knows that the maintenance man has the rifle."

"You and me. But that's enough. We'll trail him, and when he stops, you can go for help while I watch."

The truck thundered on down the rutted, winding dirt road. We reached the blacktop in time to see the back end of the panel truck disappearing over the rise. Major Kelly turned the truck onto the blacktop and floored the gas pedal. We shot up the side of the hill and, at the top, saw the panel truck a half mile ahead.

"Maybe we shouldn't get so close, sir. Won't he see us?"

"*Machts nichts*," Major Kelly said grimly. "What else should he expect to see on this road but an Army truck? He hasn't had any trouble so far. Why should he expect any?"

I didn't say anything more, but it worried me. This guy ahead of us was nobody to underestimate. And I didn't see how we could tail him all the way across the post without him suspecting something.

But that's just what we did. All the way into the center of the post on Pershing and beyond it, about nine blocks to the warehouse area. It was unfamiliar to me. I'd never even been on this part of the post. We passed the motor pool and the airfield and then we reached the rows of warehouses. There were about fifteen of the huge gray buildings, windowless and functional.

The panel truck kept to its steady twenty-five-miles an hour with us tagging along a half block behind. And I knew that this was all wrong.

"Major," I said sharply. "We can't just roll right up on him! When he stops, slow down and let me out and I'll track him on foot and you go for the CID."

"I thought you wanted to be in on the kill," he said softly; and I didn't like the smile on his face.

"I want him caught!" I said harshly. "I don't care how it's done, but I don't want it fouled up."

"We're gonna catch him, sonny. Right now."

I stared at the major's heavy, reddish face for a minute then jerked my head. What did the major think he was doing!

It was the last warehouse. The wide barnlike doors were open and the panel truck was driving inside. And our damned truck was going right in behind him!

"What do you think you're doing?" I yelled.

"You want him caught? We're going to catch him. Right now. There's two of us."

"He's got a gun!"

The major shrugged his heavy shoulders and he was smiling as if something amused him just a heck of a lot. He braked the truck to a stop a couple of feet from the back end of the panel truck.

The small truck and the bigger one almost filled the square of empty space in the center of the warehouse. On either side, stretching back into darkness, were row upon row of metal barrels holding oil. A loft ran overhead in the back half of the warehouse and rows of barrels were stacked up there, too.

It was very quiet and dim. The driver's door to the panel truck was opening.

"We can do it," the major said softly. Then he shot me a quick look. "Or are you chicken?"

My hand gripped the door handle so hard that it ached all the way up my arm. "No. I'm not chicken, but I never wanted to be a dead fool. And he's a killer. I told you about Elroy."

And with that I opened the door. The major followed suit and we both dropped to the concrete floor of the warehouse.

The maintenance man was out of his truck now and facing us. He stood curiously still. His hand was in the pocket that held the gun. In the dim light of the warehouse, I couldn't see his face. It was a white, formless blur. He didn't move or speak as the major and I came around to the front of the truck and started toward him.

"Hey, fella," the major called. "I need your help on a little detail."

I could hear the major's voice but it sounded hollow and distorted in the vastness of the warehouse. I was walking forward and somehow I was a little ahead of the major. And my throat was tight and dry and the beads of sweat were popping out all over my face. I could feel the danger. I could taste it deep in my throat.

The maintenance man stood, unmoving, absolutely quiet, and somehow, absolutely assured.

And that was wrong. All wrong. I started to turn toward Major Kelly. I half-saw the downward swing of his upraised arm in the split second before the side of my head exploded.

IN AT THE KILL

Some things you learn quickly. You don't need an ABC or even an Army manual. I knew if I moved a muscle, I'd be hurt bad again right then, so when the shoe slammed into my side I lay there as limp as a dead dog. I bit my lip until it bled and that blood mingled with the soft oozing stickiness sliding down the side of my face.

"Still breathing," Major Kelly observed. "But he's okay for a while."

"Why did you bring him here?" the other man asked angrily.

"You're damn lucky I got him to bring," Major Kelly said shortly. "I thought you were sure he went into the river last night! God, you've bungled one thing after another. We've had luck all along. Elroy can't get to the colonel at the Article 32 so he hotfoots it to me, his exec. The poor dumb fool wasn't even sure he understood right what Colonel Krueger was saying, 'cause he'd sure seen the colonel's shotgun in the gun case so did that mean the colonel hadn't taken the M-18 after all? I couldn't believe it. Our whole setup smashed because the stupid oaf looked in the colonel's gun case. But I set him up. He fell for it like a dummy when I called and told him to go into Stockton and meet the FBI. It was a cakewalk. And you've made one bungle after another."

"I didn't bungle Elroy," the other man said softly.

"No, but you sure should have gotten this kid at the same time." And he prodded me again with his shoe. "And then you steal a car and slam him over into the river—but does he end up in the river? No! He ends up in General Loring's lap. And we'd be done for if I hadn't decided to cover you this afternoon when you went to pick up the weapon."

"The general!"

"Yah, he bought this brat's idea that the M-18 never left the command post and he set a trap for us. They aren't going to blow up the command post in the morning. He made up those visiting congressmen. It was a trap and we were supposed to slip into the command post tonight to get the rifle. But the luck's still with us. Nobody was watching. The brat here was just hiding in the attic so he could be in at the kill."

Major Kelly laughed then. "He's going to be in at the kill, all right."

"What'll we do with him?"

Major Kelly didn't answer for a minute. "If he disappears," he said slowly, "the general won't know what to think. They'll tear the command post to splinters, but they won't find the rifle. I think we'll swing it yet. They may even decide the colonel was their man after all, and his scatty son just beat it because he couldn't face everybody realizing his idea about the gun in the command post was just a fairy tale. So I think we'll do the river. Weight him down. Knock out his teeth so if the body ever does come up, there won't be enough left to identify him. That's the ticket."

"When?"

"Tonight. You can get the rifle off post right now. Then tonight you can come back here and pick up the kid. We can hide his body here in the warehouse."

"You're telling me to come back," the other man said slowly. "So why me?" he demanded. "What's wrong with you doing some of the work? I fake the maintenance slip to get into the command post, I fix up the hiding place for the M-18, I kill Elroy. I'm the one who has to take the M-18 out of the attic. Pretty soon somebody's going to remember seeing a maintenance man every time something's popped and my cover'll be blown to hell."

"I am in charge of this operation," the major replied coldly. Very coldly.

"Maybe this one, but I've been an illegal in Stockton for a long time and I think control may hear a little from me on this one. If you hadn't insisted on framing Colonel Hastings with all the trimmings, we could have lifted the weapon and been done with it."

"If you take it up with control, Petrovich, we may find out rather quickly who is the most important agent. You are only an agent in place. If anyone ever questions your identity and digs deep enough, they will discover quite soon that there is no such person as Emil Gunter, that you entered this country illegally."

Major Kelly smiled, and it was the daredevil smile of a man who loves danger and intrigue. "No, Petrovich, you can't match in Moscow's eyes the value of the services of an Army officer. Who will ever question me? I'm Al Kelly, born in Houston, raised in Detroit. I'm not a fake. I'm just the most important agent the USSR has. Who else has access to the kind of classified information I'm close to? It's already set that I'll be going to the Command and General Staff College at Ft. Leavenworth on my next duty." His smile broadened. "There are quite a few secrets at Leavenworth."

The major shook his head. "I wouldn't ask control which of us is the most important, Petrovich. Really I wouldn't."

The Russian looked at him with disdain, but there was fear in his eyes, too. “Moscow should not trust a traitor like you over a good Soviet like me. I have served these many years in the U.S., far from my family and country. You are a traitor. Why do you do it? For money?”

Major Kelly laughed. The Russian’s taunts bothered him not at all. “Trying to hurt my feelings, Petrovich? You’re the fool. Devotion to duty, what does that get you?” The major shook his head again. “That’s no fun. Why do I work for your country, little man? Because it’s a game. It’s fun to outwit everybody.” The major shrugged his heavy shoulders. “And, of course, it pays well. I don’t imagine they paid you twenty-five thousand dollars for this little coup, did they? No, you’ll probably get a medal of commendation.”

The Russian didn’t answer.

“So you’d better do as you’re told, little man, or I’ll have a few words with control myself. Now, you take the rifle and deliver it to that farmhouse near Ridley. I gave you the map last week. Do you have it?”

The major’s voice was brisk again, all business. He was ready to finish up the job.

“I have the map,” Petrovich said sullenly.

“Fine. Deliver the rifle. Then return here after dark, get the kid’s body, and put it in the river. And let’s get started. I’ve got to get back to Brigade HQ before anybody notices I’ve been gone for a good while. It might get awkward when they start nosing into the kid’s disappearance.”

“As you say,” Petrovich replied. “We’d better finish him off first.”

“Have you got some wire?” Major Kelly asked. “Strangling doesn’t make a mess. And do you have something to wrap this board in?” And I knew he meant the board that he’d slammed me in the head with.

They stepped over me and went around to the back of the panel truck. I lifted my head. They couldn't see me. I heard Major Kelly saying, "And be sure to clean up the blood from the floor here."

The other man was clambering into the back of the panel truck. I struggled up on my hands and knees, and started to crawl.

About six feet away, a side aisle broke up the long line of metal barrels. I almost made it to the aisle.

"Quick, Petrovich. Get him!"

I lunged to my feet and started to run. My back tensed. I wondered if I would hear the shot before the bullet slammed into me. I risked a terrified glance over my shoulder when I reached the aisle.

Petrovich was running. In his hand I saw the glint of steel. It was a knife, not the gun. I put on another burst of speed. I realized why he held the knife. If a bullet slammed into one of those oil barrels, it might be the last bullet he'd ever shoot.

So I had a chance. Not much of one, but any chance was better than the one I'd had lying on the concrete floor of the warehouse.

And one thing about Petrovich. He might be pretty good with a knife, but he wasn't in shape. I put everything I had into that run. I was twenty feet up the aisle when he reached the opening. I ducked behind one of the rows of barrels and ran like a crab. The farther I ran the darker it got because I was running under the loft now.

A high-pitched scream shredded the quiet in the warehouse. The scream climbed higher and higher then bubbled away to nothing.

I stumbled to a stop. The sound of Petrovich's running feet stopped, too. And in the thick quiet I heard a scraping, shuffling noise from the center of the warehouse.

Slowly I raised my head until I could see.

Major Kelly's hands scratched wildly at the vise-tight fingers that encircled his throat. His legs flailed as he tried to kick behind him, but Sergeant Royce's grip held. Slowly, like a rag doll with the stuffing coming out, the major weakened.

Sergeant Royce dropped the limp body to the concrete floor and moved like a hunter toward the side aisle.

Petrovich's gun! Royce didn't know he had a gun. And Petrovich didn't need to fear an exploding barrel in that barren center patch of concrete.

I yelled it out. "Royce, he's got a gun!" But a dull plop sounded as I called. The slug caught Royce in the chest and knocked him off his feet backward with the slam of a battering ram. When his body fell to the floor, it didn't move.

Before Petrovich could turn, I was down on the floor in the narrow lane between the barrels. I crawled quickly but quietly. Tears burned in my eyes.

Sergeant Royce was a good man and a good soldier and he'd died trying to save me. Somehow, I didn't know how, he must have stashed away in the back of Major Kelly's truck. And he hadn't come out until he'd heard them plan to kill me.

He could have slipped out and gone for help. But he'd stayed and tried to save me.

The tears slipped down my face and the anger flamed inside me.

I was going to get Petrovich. Somehow, someway I was going to get him. And it was a very personal thing. I remembered Sergeant Royce and his clear quiet voice and his flowers and his faith in my Dad.

I was going to get Petrovich.

I reached another aisle cutting through the rows of barrels and I stopped to listen—and I no longer heard the sharp slap of his shoes behind me. I listened tensely and heard a click. The back end of the panel truck? What was he up to?

Cautiously I raised my head and looked over the barrels. I couldn't see him. The back end of the truck was open so he must be inside it. I looked all the way around the warehouse. Not far from me I saw a door. Could I get out and get help?

Petrovich stepped down from the back end of the truck and he was carrying something in his hands. I scuttled out into the aisle and ran. I still couldn't understand why he had stopped stalking me.

The door was locked. I looked desperately around. Just a couple of feet away a narrow wooden stairway ran up to the loft. I looked up. Barrels were stored there, too.

And I saw how I could get Petrovich.

I went up those stairs quieter than an eel through water. It was no time for him to see me. I worked my way through the rows until I reached the line of barrels right on the edge of the loft. I looked over and down.

At first I didn't understand what he was doing. He had a drill and he was drilling holes near the bottom of one of the oil barrels. The thick black oil was seeping out in small steady streams all the way around the barrel.

Every second or so, he raised his head and looked cautiously around. Making sure I wasn't creeping up on him, I realized. On the concrete close to him lay his gun and a roll of felt about two inches wide.

I was almost directly in line with him. He was about seven feet out from the edge of the loft. He drilled another hole, then sat back on his haunches and impassively watched the little black lines of oil spew out.

He picked up the roll of felt, unrolled it a couple of inches then laid the end in the pool of oil now slicking the floor. Picking up his gun, he began to back away from the oil, unrolling the felt as he went.

And I understood.

The felt, a strip about four feet long, reached its end. He laid it on the floor and pulled a packet of matches out of his pocket.

He heard the slight scraping noise at the same time I did. He looked toward the rows of barrels, hunting for me. And he lifted the gun.

But I saw his danger. Sergeant Royce, his face a white mask, was slowly crawling to his feet and I knew the immense effort, the Herculean discipline it demanded.

But Petrovich would see him. In an instant his searching gaze would move and the gun would cough and Sergeant Royce would never move again.

There was no time for my plan, no time to quietly hoist a heavy metal barrel and heave it down on Petrovich.

No time at all. Petrovich's head was moving, his hand turned. . . .

I scrambled up on top of a barrel at the edge of the loft and as I moved I yelled. Petrovich's head jerked around and his arm lifted.

I yelled as I leaped from the barrel, down, down. And Petrovich had no time. I was in the air and I could see his upturned face. And then time contracted into feeling, the burning pain that spread over my arm, the jarring thud as my feet whammed into his face, and the final sharp agony as I crashed down onto the concrete floor.

NO EASY ANSWERS

Two weeks in a hospital is enough to drive you nuts. I kept reminding myself that I was lucky to have two weeks anywhere, but the human animal has a short memory.

The warehouse and Petrovich, Major Kelly, and the pain had all receded enough that I could remember without breaking into a sweat.

The first week I hadn't been thinking about anything. I had drifted in and out of consciousness. I remember Mother's frightened face and Nancy holding my hand. I'd tried to talk, but it must have just been mumbles because I never could break through the white cloud that kept fogging over me.

But consciousness did come and the doctor was very jolly about what a hard head I had. He wasn't jolly about my leg. Everything else would heal fine in time—the split-open skin on my skull, the flesh wound in my arm from Petrovich's last wild shot, the cracked ribs. But when I'd slammed down onto him and thudded into the concrete my left leg had snapped under me. It was broken in two places, and he couldn't be sure how it would heal.

Today he was supposed to come and tell me what the latest X-rays showed. I looked at my watch. 1:30. Lunch, of course, in usual abominable hospital fashion, had been served at 11:30. The doctor was coming on his rounds after lunch.

I pushed the button that raised and lowered the bed, and sat up higher. I picked up a book and stared blankly at the cover.

Why didn't he come? Was I going to walk around with one leg shorter than the other? Was I going to walk, period?

A crisp knock sounded at the door. My voice thickened in my throat as I called out, "Come in."

And General Loring walked in.

"Sir," I said in surprise, and tried to sit up straighter.

He smiled as he walked over to the bed.

"This is the first day they'd let me in to see you," he said briskly. "I pointed out to the doctor that I held rank on my daughter, but he pointed out to me that she was good medicine and that I'd just tire you." The general laughed. "I told him he might be long on medicine but he was short on tact. Finally made it past him today, because he let me bring you the good news."

"Good news?" I scarcely dared to ask.

"Your leg's going to be fine, Bart. You'll have to work with it, of course. Therapy and plenty of patience but it's going to be all right."

I let my breath out slowly. I hadn't even realized I'd been holding it.

"And there's more good news. Your dad's promotion has come through. He's now Brigadier General Hastings. And we know who he can thank for that, son."

I shook my head. "Not just me—you and Rodriguez and Sergeant Royce. It took all of us."

"But most of all it took you," the general said quietly. "He knows it. I know it. And Sergeant Royce sure knows it. I saw him a few minutes ago. He's doing fine. Impatient to get back to work."

"Sir, can I ask you some questions?"

"Sure, Bart, fire away."

"How did Sergeant Royce pop up at the right minute?"

"The sergeant is a thinking man, Bart. He knew there wasn't any briefcase in the command post when Major Kelly came back and that was just odd enough to make him wonder. He had Rodriguez drop him off out of sight of the command post. He told Rodriguez to alert me. Then Royce angled back and hid in the rear of Major Kelly's truck. And he knew he was on to something when he heard you come out with the major."

"What did you do when Rodriguez got to you?"

"We combed the post, but the warehouses were among the last places we looked." The general shook his head. "I got to the warehouse just a few minutes after the MPs found you. I thought you were all dead. It looked like a massacre." He smiled grimly. "Colonel Griswold was very unhappy that both Petrovich and Kelly were dead."

"The sergeant and I didn't have a lot of options."

"You didn't have any options," the general said calmly. "And, as it turned out, it didn't matter that we couldn't question them." His eyes gleamed. "We found a short-wave radio set and a code-book at Petrovich's apartment in Stockton. And we really hit pay dirt at Major Kelly's quarters. He was a stamp collector and he collected some very interesting stamps—with microdots strategically applied."

"He was working on his stamps that Saturday night, when I first saw him," I said slowly.

"I'll bet he was," the general said grimly. "He was probably fixing one up to mail to another 'stamp collector'. I can't tell you too much more about it, Bart, but you've opened up leads that the FBI can follow right to the heart of the Soviet spy apparatus in this country."

"Once, when I came to, I tried to ask for the CID to tell them about Petrovich and Major Kelly, but Mother said to relax, that Sergeant Royce had already told them everything and the CID was working on it like mad."

The general nodded. "Right, and they found out a lot very quickly. Petrovich, who went under the name of Emil Gunter, was a KGB colonel. He was what's called an 'illegal' in the spy trade. He was smuggled into the U.S. Petrovich was a busy fellow. One of his chief jobs was as a provocateur to stir up civil disorders—like the mob he led against the peace march."

"Major Kelly was just a bad hat," I said tiredly.

The general nodded. "Yes. It's hard to accept it when an officer sells out. But that's what he did. And, apparently, it was just for the excitement of it and, of course, the money. The FBI has worked back and they've linked him up with some black-market racketeering in Saigon. He wasn't particular how he made his money. There's probably a lot more that we'll never know about."

I remembered the major's cold gray eyes and his good-humored face. So he'd played traitor just for the hell of it, not believing in anything, not caring whom he hurt. An amoral man. Perhaps, really, the most dangerous kind of man.

"Big fish," I said.

"Very big fish." The general looked at me soberly. "You did a good deal more than break up a spy ring and save your father's career. You've saved the lives of American soldiers in the field. If that weapon had reached Russia, its metallic content would have been analyzed and the design followed, and they would have had a rifle a good deal better than the one they now issue. And, quite quickly, their allies would have had it and one of our advantages would have been gone."

His face was grave and tired when he said, "I don't think I

need to tell you that a very small advantage can often be the difference between dying and living."

"I understand that." And I thought about Kyle. His gun had jammed. Maybe the new M-18 wouldn't jam.

"And there's just no telling what damage Kelly could have done after he reached Fort Leavenworth. I can't say anything that really expresses the debt your country owes you—except that I'm proud to know you, Bart. You are a good man. One I'd like to have in battle with me."

"Thank you, sir. Thank you very much."

"I mean that literally, Bart. There's a West Point appointment with your name on it if you'll just say the word. Your country needs men like you."

I looked up at him and for some fool reason my eyes smarted. It was the highest compliment he knew to pay.

And I thought about the great sprawling divided country that he had served for so long. He was right about one thing. It needed all of us, or it was going to go down the tubes. And I realized suddenly, passionately, that I wanted it to go on—big, rich-poor divided country—and try to reach the goals it had always honored.

Freedom. Freedom for everybody. But the wolf would always be at the door and somebody would have to beat him back. I wondered if it had to be me.

The general looked down at me and I couldn't read the expression on his face.

"You look more like Black Bart every day," he said quietly.

"The call to the colors?" I asked with a wry smile.

He shrugged. "Not really. You have to build your own life, Bart. Make your own choices. Not because your grandfather was Black Bart, but because you are Bart Hastings."

"Yes, sir." And I guess I sounded tired, because he slapped me gently on the shoulder and said, "I've overstayed. The doctor will be after me. Captain chews out general. Rest now, son."

But at the door he stopped for just a moment and said, "Get your leg well, Bart. That's the first thing, then you can decide about the Point."

And when he was gone, I lay there and stared sightlessly at the wall. Your country needs you, he had said. Maybe it did. But there are lots of ways to serve without spending your life in the Army. I knew I could be a good Army man, but I could be a lot of other things, too.

Just three weeks earlier it wouldn't have taken me ten seconds to give him an answer. But a lot had happened since the night that Nancy and I had marched through Stockton. And never again would things be as clear and simple as they had seemed that night.

No easy answers, that's what Father Rosser had said. No easy answers—not ever.

AUTHOR'S NOTE

More than 40 years have passed since the Vietnam War. The war brought riots to university campuses, weakened a generation's faith in government, and transformed America.

My husband served at Fort Leavenworth in the Judge Advocate General Corps in the early Sixties. We saw the heroism and commitment of America's military. Back in civilian life, we saw the mounting casualties and agreed with millions of Americans that the seemingly endless slaughter had to end.

There was heartbreak and passion on both sides and that is the story I wanted to tell in *No Easy Answers*.

There are never easy answers when government appears indifferent to its citizens. May Americans always celebrate freedom and never forget those who serve her in the military.

ABOUT THE AUTHOR

Carolyn Hart, an accomplished master of mystery, is the author of twenty previous Death on Demand novels. Her books have won multiple Agatha, Anthony, and Macavity Awards. She is also the creator of the Henrie O series which features a retired reporter, and the Bailey Ruth series which stars an impetuous, redheaded ghost. One of the founders of Sisters in Crime, Hart lives in Oklahoma City.

ABOUT THE AUTHOR

CAROLYN HART CLASSICS

FROM OPEN ROAD MEDIA

www.ingramcontent.com/pod-product-compliance
Lightning Source LLC
LaVergne TN
LVHW090607110826
845146LV00001B/290

9798337203980